THE LAST WORD AND OTHER STORIES

Graham Greene

THE LAST WORD

and other stories

LESTER
&ORPEN
DENNYS
PUBLISHERS

FIRST EDITION

Published simultaneously by
Lester & Orpen Dennys in Canada,
and by Reinhardt Books in the United Kingdom.

Canadian Cataloguing in Publication Data ·

Greene, Graham, *1904*–
The last word and other stories

1st Canadian ed.
ISBN 0-88619-366-4 (bound) ISBN 0-88619-323-0 (pbk.)

I. Title.

PR6013.R44L38 1990   823'.912   C90-093644-4

Printed and bound in the U.K. for

Lester & Orpen Dennys
78 Sullivan Street, Toronto, Canada
M5T 1C1

CONTENTS

The stories included in this volume first appeared in the following publications: *Collier's*, 'The Lieutenant Died Last', 1940; *Graphic*, 'Murder for the Wrong Reason', 1929; *Independent*, 'The Last Word', 1988, 'The Moment of Truth', 1988, 'An Old Man's Memory', 1989; *Oxford Outlook*, 'The New House', 1923; *Punch*, 'Work Not in Progress', 1955, 'The Man who Stole the Eiffel Tower', 1956; *Strand*, 'The News in English', 1940, 'The Lottery Ticket', 1947.

'An Appointment with the General' was published in *Firebird*, 1982, under the title 'On the Way Back: a work not in progress'.

'A Branch of the Service' is published here for the first time.

Here are a few notes to this collection of stories dating from 1923–89 of which only four have appeared before in book form and none of which are included in *Collected Short Stories*, published in 1972.

Why did I exclude 'The News in English' and 'The Lieutenant Died Last' from that volume? It was not that I thought them unworthy to appear. It was because Time (and with it Memory) passes with horrifying speed. How many people below the age of sixty would remember Lord Haw-Haw, whom I listened to nightly in 1940 on the radio, and understand the title and subject of 'The News in English'? In that war, they might well ask, was it plausible for a squad of foreign soldiers to descend by parachute on an English village? None had occurred in the German war and we had been engaged in at least three conflicts since then. The questions are even more relevant today than in 1967, but I am taking the risk of reprinting because I like the stories, and my friend Cavalcanti made a film of 'The Lieutenant Died Last' which I regret never having seen, for I was out of England on wartime duties when it was shown.

'The Lottery Ticket' was included in a volume called *Nineteen Stories* in 1947 but excluded from *Twenty-One Stories* in 1954. I thought then that there were too many echoes in it of *The Lawless Roads* and *The Power and the*

Glory. Well, those two books today belong to an even more distant past, so I have decided to give 'The Lottery Ticket' a second chance.

I would like too to explain the digging up from a magazine of the twenties of a detective story, 'Murder for the Wrong Reason'. Reading it more than sixty years later, I found that I couldn't detect the murderer before he was disclosed.

During those early years in the twenties and thirties I was much interested in the detective story (I even began *Brighton Rock* expecting it to be a detective story), and I have dim memories of a detective novel which I began and abandoned in the early thirties, containing a priest as detective and a child in her early teens as the killer.

The earliest story in this volume, 'The New House', was published in 1929 in the *Oxford Outlook*. Why was it ever published, some may reasonably ask? The answer is a very simple one – I was the editor of the *Outlook*.

THE LAST WORD AND OTHER STORIES

The Last Word

The old man was only a little surprised, because he was by now well accustomed to inexplicable events, when he received at the hands of a stranger a passport in a name which was not his own, a visa and an exit permit for a country which he had never expected or even desired to visit. He was indeed very old, and he was accustomed to the narrow life he had led alone without human contacts: he had even found a kind of happiness in deprivation. He had a single room to live and sleep in: a small kitchen and a bathroom. Once a month there came a small but sufficient pension which arrived from Somewhere, but he didn't know where. Perhaps it was connected with the accident years before which had robbed him of his memory. All that had remained in his mind of that occasion was a sharp noise, a flash like lightning and then a long darkness full of confusing dreams from which he finally woke in the same small room that he lived in now.

'You will be fetched at the airport on the 25th,' the stranger told him, 'and be taken to your plane. At the other end you will be met and a room is ready for you. It would be best for you if you spoke to no one on the plane.'

'The 25th? This is December, isn't it?' He found it difficult to keep account of time.

'Of course.'

'Then it will be Christmas Day.'

'Christmas Day was abolished more than twenty years ago. After your accident.'

He was left wondering – how does one abolish a day? When the man left he looked up, half expecting an answer, to a small wooden crucifix which hung over his bed. One arm of the cross and with it one arm of the figure had been broken off – he had found it two years before – or was it three? – in the dustbin which he shared with his neighbours who never spoke to him. He said aloud, 'And you? Have they abolished you?' The missing arm seemed to give him the answer, 'Yes.' There was in a way a communication between them as though they shared a memory between them.

With his neighbours there was no communication. Since he had returned to life in this room he had not spoken to one of them, for he could feel that they were afraid to speak to him. It was as if they knew something about him which he didn't know himself. Perhaps a crime committed before the darkness fell. There was always a man in the street who could not be regarded as a neighbour, for he was changed every other day, and he too spoke to no one at all, not even to the old lady on the top floor who was inclined to gossip. Once in the street she had used the name – not the name on the passport – with a sideways look which took in both of them – the old man and the watcher. It was a common enough name, John.

Once, perhaps because the day was warm and bright after weeks of rain, the old man had ventured a remark to the man in the street as he went to fetch his bread, 'God bless you, my dear fellow', and the man winced as though struck by a sudden pain and turned his back. The old man went on to fetch his bread which was his staple food and he had long been aware that he was followed to the shop. The whole atmosphere was a bit mysterious, but he was not deeply disturbed. Once he remarked to his only audience, the damaged wooden figure, 'I think they want to leave you and me alone.' He was quite content, as though somewhere in the dark forgotten past he had suffered an immense burden from which he was now free.

The day which he still thought of as Christmas arrived and so did the stranger – 'To take you to the airport. Have you finished packing?'

'I haven't much to pack and I have no case.'

'I will fetch one,' and so he did. While he was gone the old man wrapped the wooden figure in his only spare jacket which he put in the case as soon as it was brought and covered it with two shirts and some under-clothes.

'Is that all you have?'

'At my age one needs very little.'

'What are you carrying in your pocket?'

'Only a book.'

'Let me see it.'

'Why?'

'I have my orders.'

He snatched it from the old man's hand and looked at the title page.

'You have no right to this. How did it come into your possession?'

'I have had it since childhood.'

'They should have seized it in the hospital. I will have to report this.'

'No one is to blame. I kept it hidden.'

'You were brought in unconscious. You weren't capable of hiding.'

'I expect they were too busy saving my life.'

'I call it criminal carelessness.'

'I think I remember someone did ask me what it was. I told them the truth. A book of ancient history.'

'Forbidden history. This will go to the incinerator.'

'It's not so important,' the old man said. 'Read a little of it first. You will see.'

'I shall do no such thing. I am loyal to the General.'

'Oh, you are right of course. Loyalty is a great virtue. But don't worry. I haven't read much of it for some years. My favourite passages are here in my head, and you can't incinerate my head.'

'Don't be too sure of that,' the man replied. They were his last words before they reached the airport, and there everything strangely changed.

2

An officer in uniform greeted the old man with such great courtesy that he felt as though he were returning to a very distant past. The officer even gave him a military salute. He said, 'The General asked me to wish you a comfortable journey.'

'Where are you taking me?'

The officer made no reply to his question, but asked the civilian guard, 'Is this all his luggage?'

'All, but I took away this book.'

'Let me see it.' The officer turned to the title page. 'Of course,' he said, 'you were doing your duty, but all the same give it him back. These are special circumstances. He is the guest of the General, and anyway there's no danger in a book like this now.'

'The law...'

'Even laws can become out of date.'

The old man repeated his question in another form. 'What line am I travelling on?'

'You too, sir, are a little out of date. There is only one line now – The World United.'

'Oh dear, oh dear, what changes there have been.'

'Don't worry, sir, the time of change is over. The world is settled and at peace. No need for change.'

'Where are you taking me?'

'Only to another province. A mere four hours' flight. In the General's own plane.'

It was an extraordinary plane. There was what one might call a sitting-room with ample armchairs, sufficient for only six people, so that they could be transformed into beds: through an open door as they passed he could see a bath – he hadn't seen a bath for years (his small studio had only a shower) and he felt a strong desire to spend the hours which followed stretched out in the warm water. A bar separated the chairs from the cockpit, and an almost cringing steward offered him a choice from what appeared to be the drinks of all nations, if one could speak of all nations in this United World. Even his poor clothes did not seem to diminish the steward's respect. Presumably he cringed to any guest of the General however unsuitable he might think one to be.

(7)

The officer took his seat at some distance as though he wished to leave him discreetly at peace with his forbidden book, but what he felt was a deeper desire for the peace and the silence. He was tired out by the mystery of things: the mystery of the small studio which he had left, of the tension coming from God knew where, of this luxury plane and above all of the bath . . . His mind, as it so often did, went in pursuit of his memory, which stopped abruptly at this startling crack of sound and the darkness which followed it . . . how many years ago? It was as if he had been living under a total anaesthetic which was only now beginning to wear thin. Suddenly he was frightened in this great private plane of what memories might await him if he woke. He began to read his book; it opened automatically from long use at a passage he knew by heart: 'He was in the world and the world was made by him and the world knew him not.'

The steward's voice sounded in his ear, 'A little caviare, sir, or a glass of vodka, or would you prefer a glass of dry white wine?'

Without looking up from the familiar page he said, 'No, no thank you. I am not hungry or thirsty.'

The clink of the glass the steward removed brought back a memory. His hand of its own accord tried to lay down something on the table before him, and for a moment in front of him he saw a host of strangers with bowed heads, there was a deep silence and then came that startling crack and the darkness which followed . . .

The steward's voice woke him. 'Your safety belt, sir. We shall be arriving in five minutes.'

(8)

3

Another officer awaited him at the bottom of the steps and led him towards a large car. The ceremony, the courtesy, the luxury stirred the hidden memories. He felt no surprise now: it was as though he had experienced all this many years before: he gave mechanically a deprecating movement to the hand and a phrase slipped from his mouth, 'I am a servant of the servants' and remained unfinished as the door slammed.

They drove through streets which were empty except for a few queues outside certain stores. He began to say again, 'I am a servant.' Outside the hotel the manager was awaiting them. He bowed and told the old man, 'I am proud to receive a personal guest of the General. I hope you will have every comfort during your short stay here. You have only to ask . . .'

The old man looked up with astonishment at the fourteen floors. He asked, 'For how long are you keeping me here?'

'You are booked, sir, for one night.'

The officer broke hastily in, 'So that you may see the General tomorrow. He wants you to have a good rest tonight after your journey.'

The old man searched his memory and a name came back. It was as though memory were returning to him in broken pieces. 'General Megrim?'

'No, no. General Megrim died nearly twenty years ago.'

A uniformed doorkeeper saluted him as they entered the hotel. The concierge was ready with the keys. The officer said, 'I will leave you here, sir, and tomorrow morning I will come to fetch you at 11. The General will see you at 11.30.'

The manager accompanied him to the lift.

After they had both gone safely away the concierge turned to the officer. 'Who is this gentleman? The guest of the General? He looks a very poor man from his clothes.'

'He's the Pope.'

'The Pope? What's the Pope?' the concierge asked, but the officer left the hotel without making any reply.

4

When the manager left him the old man was aware of how tired he was, but all the same he examined his surroundings with astonishment. He even felt the deep succulent mattress of the great double bed. He opened the door of the bathroom and saw an array of little bottles. The only thing he bothered to unpack was the wooden statuette he had so carefully hidden. He propped it up against the mirror on the dressing-table. He threw his clothes on a chair and then as though obeying an order lay down on the bed. If he had understood anything of what was happening, perhaps he would have found it impossible to sleep, but understanding nothing he was able to sink down on the deep mattress, where sleep came immediately, and with it a dream, parts of which he remembered on waking.

He had been talking – he saw it all clearly – in some sort of immense barn to an audience of not more than a few dozen people. On one wall hung a mutilated wooden cross and a figure without an arm, like the one hidden in his case. He couldn't remember what he had been saying, for the words were in a language – or several languages – which he didn't know or couldn't remember. The barn slowly decreased in size until it was no larger than the little studio which he had left, and in front of him knelt one old woman with a small girl beside her. *She* did not kneel, but looked at him with a look of contempt which seemed to express a thought as clearly as if she had spoken aloud, 'I don't understand a word you're saying and why can't you speak properly?'

He woke to a terrible sense of failure and lay awake on his bed desperately trying to find a way back into the dream and utter some words which the child might understand. He even tried out a few of them at random. 'Pax,' he said aloud, but that would be as foreign a word to her as it had been to him. He tried another, 'Love'. It came more easily to his lips, but it seemed to him now too commonplace a word with its contradictory meaning. He found that he didn't really know what it meant himself. It was something he was not sure he had ever experienced. Perhaps – before the strange crack in the darkness which followed – he might have had a hint, but surely if love had any real importance a small memory of it would have survived.

His uneasy thoughts were interrupted by the entrance of a waiter who brought him a tray with coffee and a variety of breads and croissants he had never seen at the small bakery which served him with the only meals he took.

'The colonel asked me to remind you, sir, that he will be here at 11 to take you to the General and that your clothes for the occasion are in the wardrobe. In case you forgot to pack them in your rather hurried departure you will find razor and brushes and all that is required in the bathroom.'

'My clothes are on the chair,' he told the waiter and he added a friendly joke, 'I didn't come here quite naked.'

'I have been told to take them away. All you require is there,' and he pointed at the wardrobe.

The old man looked at his jacket and trousers, his shirt, socks, and not for the first time, as the waiter picked them gingerly up, the thought came to him that they were indeed in need of a wash. He had seen no reason in all the last years to waste a little of his small pension at the cleaners when the only people who saw him regularly were the baker, the men sent to watch him and occasionally a neighbour who would avoid looking in his direction and even cross the street to avoid him. Clean clothes might be a social need for others, but he had no social life.

The waiter left him and he stood in his underpants brooding on the mystery of things. Then there was a knock on the door and the officer who had brought him entered.

'But you're not dressed yet, and you've eaten nothing. The General expects us to be on time.'

'The waiter has taken my clothes.'

'Your clothes are in the wardrobe.' He flung the door open and the old man saw a white surplice and a white cape hanging there. He said, 'Why? What are you asking? I have no right . . .'

'The General wishes to do you honour. He will be in full dress uniform himself. There is even a guard of

(12)

honour waiting for you. You must wear your uniform too.'

'My uniform?'

'Be quick and shave. There will almost certainly be photographs for the world's press. The United World Press.'

He obeyed and in his confusion cut himself in several places. Then unwillingly he put on his white robe and the cape. There was a long mirror on the wardrobe door and he exclaimed with horror, 'I look like a priest.'

'You were a priest. These robes have been lent by the World Museum of Myths for the occasion. Hold out your hand.'

He obeyed. Authority had spoken. The officer slipped a ring on one of his fingers. 'The Museum,' he said, 'was reluctant to lend us the ring, but the General insisted. This is an occasion which will never be repeated. Follow me please.' As they were about to leave the wooden object on the dressing-table caught his eye. He said, 'They should never have allowed you to bring that with you.'

The old man had no wish to bring trouble to anyone. 'I hid it carefully,' he said.

'Never mind. I dare say the Museum will be glad to have it.'

'I want to keep it.'

'I don't think you will need it after you have seen the General.'

5

They drove through many strangely empty streets before they reached a great square. In front of what might once have been a palace a line of soldiers was drawn up and there the car stopped. The officer told him, 'We descend here. Don't be alarmed. The General wants to show you proper military honours as a former head of state.'

'Head of state? I don't understand.'

'Please. After you.'

The old man would have tripped on his robe if the officer had not grasped his arm. As he straightened there was a crash of sound and he nearly fell again. It was as though that sharp crack which he had heard once, before the long darkness wrapped him in its folds, was now multiplied a dozen times. The crash seemed to break his head in two and into that gap the memories of a lifetime began to pour in. He repeated, 'I don't understand.'

'In your honour.'

He looked down at his feet and saw the fold of the surplice. He looked at his hand and saw the ring. There was a clash of metal. The soldiers were presenting arms.

6

The General greeted him with courtesy and came directly to the point. He said, 'I want you to understand that I was in no way responsible for the attempt to kill you. It was a grave mistake by one of my predecessors, a General Megrim. Such mistakes are easily made in the later stages of a revolution. It has taken us a hundred years to establish the world state and world peace. In his way he was afraid of you and the few followers you still had.'

'Afraid of me?'

'Yes. You must realize that your Church has been

responsible throughout history for many wars. At last we have abolished war.'

'But you are a General. I saw outside a number of soldiers.'

'They remain as the preservers of world peace. Perhaps in another hundred years they will cease to exist just as your Church has ceased to exist.'

'Has it ceased to exist? My memory failed me a long time ago.'

'You are the last living Christian,' the General said. 'You are an historic figure. For that reason I wanted to honour you at the end.'

The General took out a cigarette case and offered it. 'Will you smoke with me, Pope John. I'm sorry I forgot the number. Was it XXIX?'

'Pope? I'm sorry I don't smoke. Why do you call me Pope?'

'The last Pope but still a Pope.' The General lit a cigarette and continued. 'You must understand we have nothing at all against you personally. You occupied a great position. We shared many of the same ambitions. We had a great deal in common. That was one of the reasons why General Megrim considered you a dangerous enemy. You represented, as long as you had followers, an alternative choice. As long as there was an alternative choice there would always be war. I don't agree with the method which he took. To shoot you in such a clandestine way as you were saying – what do you call it?'

'My prayers?'

'No, no. It was a public ceremony already forbidden by law.'

(15)

The old man felt himself at a loss. 'The Mass?' he asked.

'Yes, yes, I think that was the word. The trouble with what he arranged was that it might have turned you into a martyr and delayed our programme not a little. It's true that there were only a dozen people at that – what do you call it? – Mass. But his method was risky. General Megrim's successor realized that, and I have followed the same quieter line. We have kept you alive. We have never allowed the press to make even an occasional reference to you, or to your quiet life in retirement.'

'I don't altogether understand. You must forgive me. I'm only beginning to remember. When your soldiers fired just now . . .'

'We preserved you because you were the last leader of those who still called themselves Christians. The others gave up without too much difficulty. What a strange pack of names – Jehovah's Witnesses, Lutherans, Calvinists, Anglicans. They all died away one by one with the years. Your lot called themselves Catholic as though they claimed to represent the whole bunch even while they fought them. Historically I suppose you were the first to organize yourselves and claim to follow that mythical Jewish carpenter.'

The old man said, 'I wonder how his arm got broken.'

'His arm?'

'I'm sorry. My mind was wandering.'

'We left what was left of you to the last because you still had a few followers and because we did have certain aims in common. World peace, the destruction of poverty. There was a period when we could use you. Use you to

(16)

destroy the idea of national countries for the sake of a greater whole. You had ceased to be a real danger, which made General Megrim's action unnecessary – or at any rate premature. Now we are satisfied that all this nonsense is finished, forgotten. You have no followers, Pope John. I have had you watched closely over the last twenty years. Not a single person has tried to contact you. You have no power and the world is one and at peace. You are no longer an enemy to be feared. I am sorry for you, for they must have been very long and tedious years in that lodging of yours. In a way a faith is like old age. It can't go on forever. Communism grew old and died, so did imperialism. Christianity is dead too except for you. I expect you were a good Pope as popes go, and I want to do you the honour of no longer keeping you in these dreary conditions.'

'You are kind. They were not so dreary as you think. I had a friend with me. I could talk to him.'

'What on earth do you mean? You were alone. Even when you went out of your door to buy bread you were alone.'

'He was waiting for me when I came back. I wish his arm had not been broken.'

'Oh, you are talking about that wooden image. The Museum of Myths will be glad to add it to its collection. But the time has come to talk of serious things, not of myths. You see this weapon I am putting on my desk. I don't believe in people being allowed to suffer unnecessarily. I respect you. I am not General Megrim. I want you to die with dignity. The last Christian. This is a moment of history.'

'You intend to kill me?'

'Yes.'

It was relief the old man felt, not fear. He said, 'You will be sending me where I've often wanted to go during the last twenty years.'

'Into darkness?'

'Oh, the darkness I have known was not death. Just an absence of light. You are sending me into the light. I am grateful to you.'

'I had hoped you would take a last meal with me. As a kind of symbol. A symbol of final friendship between two born to be enemies.'

'Forgive me, but I am not hungry. Let the execution go ahead.'

'At least, take a glass of wine with me, Pope John.'

'Thank you. I will take that.'

The General poured out two glasses. His hand shook a little as he drained his glass. The old man raised his as though in salute. He said in a low voice some words which the General could not properly catch, in a language which he did not understand. 'Corpus domini nostri . . .' As his last Christian enemy drank, he fired.

Between the pressure on the trigger and the bullet exploding a strange and frightening doubt crossed his mind: is it possible that what this man believed may be true?

The News in English

Tonight Lord Haw-Haw of Zeesen was off the air.

All over England the new voice was noticed; precise and rather lifeless, it was the voice of a typical English don.

In his first broadcast he referred to himself as a man young enough to sympathize with what he called 'the resurgence of youth all over the new Germany', and that was the reason – combined with the pedantic tone – he was at once nicknamed Dr Funkhole.

It is the tragedy of such men that they are never alone in the world.

Old Mrs Bishop was knitting by the fire at her house in Crowborough when young Mrs Bishop tuned in to Zeesen. The sock was khaki: it was as if she had picked up at the point where she had dropped a stitch in 1918. The grim comfortable house stood in one of the long avenues, all spruce and laurel and a coating of snow, which are used to nothing but the footsteps of old retired people. Young Mrs Bishop never forgot that moment; the wind beating up across Ashdown Forest against the blacked-out window, and her mother-in-law happily knitting, and the sense of everything waiting for this moment. Then the voice came into the room from Zeesen in the middle of a sentence, and old Mrs Bishop said firmly, 'That's David.'

Young Mary Bishop made a hopeless protest – 'It can't be,' but she knew.

'I know my son if you don't know your husband.'

It seemed incredible that the man speaking couldn't

THE NEWS IN ENGLISH

hear them, that he should just go on, reiterating for the
hundredth time the old lies, as if there were nobody
anywhere in the world who knew him – a wife or a
mother.

Old Mrs Bishop had stopped knitting. She said, 'Is that
the man they've been writing about – Doctor Funkhole?'

'It must be.'

'It's David.'

The voice was extraordinarily convincing: he was going
into exact engineering details – David Bishop had been a
mathematics don at Oxford. Mary Bishop twisted the
wireless off and sat down beside her mother-in-law.

'They'll want to know who it is,' Mrs Bishop said.

'We mustn't tell them,' said Mary.

The old fingers had begun on the khaki sock. She said,
'It's our duty.' Duty, it seemed to Mary Bishop, was a
disease you caught with age: you ceased to feel the tug-tug
of personal ties; you gave yourself up to the great tides
of patriotism and hate. She said, 'They must have made
him do it. We don't know what threats – '

'That's neither here nor there.'

She gave weakly in to hopeless wishes. 'If only he'd got
away in time. I never wanted him to give that lecture
course.'

'He always was stubborn,' said old Mrs Bishop.

'He said there wouldn't be a war.'

'Give me the telephone.'

'But you see what it means,' said Mary Bishop. 'He
may be tried for treason if we win.'

'*When* we win,' old Mrs Bishop said.

*

The nickname was not altered, even after the interviews with the two Mrs Bishops, even after the sub-acid derogatory little article about David Bishop's previous career. It was suggested now that he had known all along that war was coming, that he had gone to Germany to evade military service, leaving his wife and his mother to be bombed. Mary Bishop fought, almost in vain, with the reporters for some recognition that he might have been forced – by threats or even physical violence. The most one paper would admit was that if threats had been used Bishop had taken a very unheroic way out. We praise heroes as though they are rare, and yet we are always ready to blame another man for lack of heroism. The name Dr Funkhole stuck.

But the worst of it to Mary Bishop was old Mrs Bishop's attitude. She turned a knife in the wound every evening at 9.15. The radio set must be tuned in to Zeesen, and there she sat listening to her son's voice and knitting socks for some unknown soldier on the Maginot Line. To young Mrs Bishop none of it made sense – least of all that flat, pedantic voice with its smooth, well-thought-out, elaborate lies. She was afraid to go out now into Crowborough: the whispers in the post office, the old faces watching her covertly in the library. Sometimes she thought almost with hatred, *why has David done this to me? Why?*

Then suddenly she got her answer.

The voice for once broke new ground. It said, 'Somewhere back in England my wife may be listening to me. I am a stranger to the rest of you, but she knows that I am not in the habit of lying.'

A personal appeal was too much. Mary Bishop had faced her mother-in-law and the reporters – she couldn't face her husband. She began to cry, sitting close beside the radio set like a child beside its doll's house when something has been broken in it which nobody can repair. She heard the voice of her husband speaking as if he were at her elbow from a country which was now as distant and as inaccessible as another planet.

'The fact of the matter is – '

The words came slowly out as if he were emphasizing a point in a lecture, and then he went on – to what would concern a wife. The low price of food, the quantity of meat in the shops. He went into great detail, giving figures, picking out odd, irrelevant things – like Mandarin oranges and toy zebras – perhaps to give an effect of richness and variety.

Suddenly Mary Bishop sat up with a jerk as if she had been asleep. She said, 'Oh, God, where's that pencil?' and upset one of the too many ornaments looking for one. Then she began to write, but in no time at all the voice was saying, 'Thank you for having listened to me so attentively,' and Zeesen had died out on the air. She said, 'Too late.'

'What's too late?' said old Mrs Bishop sharply. 'Why did you want a pencil?'

'Just an idea,' Mary Bishop said.

She was led next day up and down the cold, unheated corridors of a War Office in which half the rooms were empty, evacuated. Oddly enough, her relationship to David Bishop was of use to her now, if only because it evoked some curiosity and a little pity. But she no longer wanted the pity, and at last she reached the right man.

He listened to her with great politeness. He was not in uniform. His rather good tweeds made him look as if he had just come up from the country for a day or two, to attend to the war. When she had finished he said, 'It's rather a tall story, you know, Mrs Bishop. Of course it's been a great shock to you – this – well – action of your husband's.'

'I'm proud of it.'

'Just because in the old days you had this – scheme, you really believe – ?'

'If he was away from me and he telephoned "The fact of the matter is," it always meant, "This is all lies, but take the initial letters which follow." . . . Oh, Colonel, if you only knew the number of unhappy weekends I've saved him from – because, you see, he could always telephone to me, even in front of his host.' She said with tears in her voice, 'Then I'd send him a telegram . . .'

'Yes. But still – you didn't get anything this time, did you?'

'I was too late. I hadn't a pencil. I only got this – I know it doesn't seem to make sense.' She pushed the paper across. S O S P I C. I know it might easily be coincidence – that it does seem to make a kind of word.'

'An odd word.'

'Mightn't it be a man's name?'

The officer in tweeds was looking at it, she suddenly realized, with real interest – as if it was a rare kind of pheasant. He said, 'Excuse me a moment,' and left her. She could hear him telephoning to somebody from another room: the little ting of the bell, silence, and then a low voice she couldn't overhear. Then he returned, and she could tell at once from his face that all was well.

He sat down and fiddled with a fountain-pen – he was obviously embarrassed. He started a sentence and stopped it. Then he brought out in an embarrassed gulp, 'We'll have to apologize to your husband.'

'It meant something?'

He was obviously making his mind up about something difficult and out of the way – he was not in the habit of confiding in members of the public. But she had ceased to be a member of the public.

'My dear Mrs Bishop,' he said, 'I've got to ask a great deal from you.'

'Of course. Anything.'

He seemed to reach a decision and stopped fiddling. 'A neutral ship called the *Pic* was sunk this morning at 4.00 a.m., with a loss of two hundred lives. SOS *Pic*. If we'd had your husband's warning, we could have got destroyers to her in time. I've been speaking to the Admiralty.'

Mary Bishop said in a tone of fury, 'The things they are writing about David. Is there one of them who'd have the courage – ?'

'That's the worst part of it, Mrs Bishop. They must go on writing. Nobody must know, except my department and yourself.'

'His mother?'

'You mustn't even tell her.'

'But can't you make them just leave him alone?'

'This afternoon I shall ask them to intensify their

campaign – in order to discourage others. An article on the legal aspect of treason.'

'And if I refuse to keep quiet?'

'Your husband's life won't be worth much, will it?'

'So he's just got to go on?'

'Yes. Just go on.'

He went on for four weeks. Every night now she tuned in to Zeesen with a new horror – that he would be off the air. The code was a child's code. How could they fail to detect it? But they did fail. Men with complicated minds can be deceived by simplicity. And every night, too, she had to listen to her mother-in-law's indictment; every episode which she thought discreditable out of a child's past was brought out – the tiniest incident. Women in the last war had found a kind of pride in 'giving' their sons: this, too, was a gift on the altar of a warped patriotism. But now young Mrs Bishop didn't cry: she just held on – it was relief enough to hear his voice.

It wasn't often that he had information to give – the phrase 'the fact of the matter is' was a rare one in his talks. Sometimes there were the numbers of the regiments passing through Berlin, or of men on leave – very small details, which might be of value to military intelligence, but to her seemed hardly worth the risk of a life. If this was all he could do, why, why hadn't he allowed them simply to intern him?

At last she could bear it no longer. She visited the War Office again. The man in tweeds was still there, but this time for some reason he was wearing a black tail coat and a black stock as if he had been to a funeral. He must have been to a funeral, and she thought with more fear than ever of her husband.

'He's a brave man, Mrs Bishop,' he said.

'You needn't tell me that,' she cried bitterly.

'We shall see that he gets the highest possible decoration . . .'

'Decorations!'

'What do you want, Mrs Bishop? He's doing his duty.'

'So are other men. But they come home on leave. Sometime. He can't go on for ever. Soon they are bound to find out.'

'What can we do?'

'You can get him out of there. Hasn't he done enough for you?'

He said gently, 'It's beyond our power. How can we communicate with him?'

'Surely you have agents.'

'Two lives would be lost. Can't you imagine how they watch him?'

Yes. She could imagine all that clearly. She had spent too many holidays in Germany – as the Press had not failed to discover – not to know how men were watched, telephone lines tapped, table companions scrutinized.

He said, 'If there was some way we could get a message to him, it *might* be managed. We do owe him that.'

Young Mrs Bishop said quickly before he could change his mind, 'Well, the code works both ways. The fact of the matter is – ! We have news broadcast in German. He might one day listen in.'

'Yes. There's a chance.'

She became privy to the plan because again they needed

her help. They wanted to attract his notice first by some phrase peculiar to her. For years they had spoken German together on their annual holiday. That phrase was to be varied in every broadcast, and elaborately they worked out a series of messages which would convey to him the same instructions – to go to a certain station on the Cologne–Wesel line and contact there a railway worker who had already helped five men and two women to escape from Germany.

Mary Bishop felt she knew the place well – the small country station which probably served only a few dozen houses and a big hotel where people went in the old days for cures. The opportunity was offered him, if he could only take it, by an elaborate account of a railway accident at that point – so many people killed – sabotage – arrests. It was plugged in the news as relentlessly as the Germans repeated the news of false sinkings, and they answered indignantly back that there had been no accident.

It seemed more horrible than ever to Mary Bishop – those nightly broadcasts from Zeesen. The voice was in the room with her, and yet he couldn't know whether any message for which he risked his life reached home, and she couldn't know whether their message to him just petered out unheard or unrecognized.

Old Mrs Bishop said, 'Well, we can do without David tonight, I should hope.' It was a new turn in her bitterness – now she would simply wipe him off the air. Mary Bishop protested. She said she must hear – then at least she would know that he was well.

'It serves him right if he's not well.'

'I'm going to listen,' Mary Bishop persisted.

'Then I'll go out of the room. I'm tired of his lies.'

'You're his mother, aren't you?'

'That's not my fault. I didn't choose – like you did. I tell you I won't listen to it.'

Mary Bishop turned the knob. 'Then stop your ears,' she cried in a sudden fury, and heard David's voice coming over.

'The lies,' he was saying, 'put over by the British capitalist Press. There has not even been a railway accident – leave alone any sabotage – at the place so persistently mentioned in the broadcasts from England. Tomorrow I am leaving myself for the so-called scene of the accident, and I propose in my broadcast the day after tomorrow to give you an impartial observer's report, with records of the very railwaymen who are said to have been shot for sabotage. Tomorrow, therefore, I shall not be on the air . . .'

'Oh, thank God, thank God,' Mary Bishop said.

The old woman grumbled by the fire. 'You haven't much to thank Him for.'

All next day she found herself praying, although she didn't much believe in prayer. She visualized that station 'on the Rhine not far from Wesel' – and not far either from the Dutch frontier. There must be some method of getting across – with the help of that unknown worker – possibly in a refrigerating van. No idea was too fantastic to be true. Others had succeeded before him.

All through the day she tried to keep pace with him – he would have to leave early, and she imagined his cup of ersatz coffee and the slow wartime train taking him south and west. She thought of his fear and of his excitement – he was coming home to her. Ah, when he landed safely, what a day that would be! The papers then would have to eat their words – no more Dr Funkhole and no more of this place, side by side with his unloving mother.

At midday, she thought, he has arrived: he has his black discs with him to record the men's voices, he is probably watched, but he will find his chance – and now he is not alone. He has someone with him helping him. In one way or another he will miss his train home. The freight train will draw in – perhaps a signal will stop it outside the station. She saw it all so vividly, as the early winter dark came down and she blacked the windows out, that she found herself thankful he possessed, as she knew, a white mackintosh. He would be less visible waiting there in the snow.

Her imagination took wings, and by dinnertime she felt sure that he was already on the way to the frontier. That night there was no broadcast from Dr Funkhole, and she sang as she bathed and old Mrs Bishop beat furiously on her bedroom floor above.

In bed she could almost feel herself vibrating with the heavy movement of *his* train. She saw the landscape going by outside – there must be a crack in any van in which he lay hid, so that he could mark the distances. It was very much the landscape of Crowborough – spruces powdered with snow, the wide dreary waste they called a forest, dark avenues – she fell asleep.

When she woke she was still happy. Perhaps before night she would receive a cable from Holland, but if it didn't come she would not be anxious because so many things in wartime might delay it. It didn't come.

That night she made no attempt to turn on the radio, so old Mrs Bishop changed her tactics again. 'Well,' she said, 'aren't you going to listen to your husband?'

'He won't be broadcasting.' Very soon now she could turn on his mother in triumph and say, *There, I knew it all the time, my husband's a hero.*

'That was last night.'

'He won't be broadcasting again.'

'What do you mean? Turn it on and let me hear.'

There was no harm in proving that she knew – she turned it on.

A voice was talking in German – something about an accident and English lies, she didn't bother to listen. She felt too happy. 'There,' she said, 'I told you. It's not David.'

And then David spoke.

He said, 'You have been listening to the actual voices of the men your English broadcasters have told you were shot by the German police. Perhaps now you will be less inclined to believe the exaggerated stories you hear of life inside Germany today.'

'There,' old Mrs Bishop said, 'I told you.'

And all the world, she thought, *will go on telling me now, for ever – Dr Funkhole. He never got those messages. He's there for keeps.* David's voice said with curious haste and harshness, 'The fact of the matter is – '

He spoke rapidly for about two minutes as if he were afraid they would fade him at any moment, and yet it sounded harmless enough – the old stories about plentiful food and how much you could buy for an English pound – figures. But some of the examples this time, she thought with dread, are surely so fantastic that even the German brain will realize something is wrong. How had he ever dared to show this copy to his chiefs?

She could hardly keep pace with her pencil, so rapidly did he speak. The words grouped themselves on her pad: *Five U's refuelling hodie noon 53.23 by 10.5. News reliable source Wesel so returned. Talk unauthorized. The end.*

'This order. Many young wives I feel enjoy giving one' – he hesitated – 'one's day's butter in every dozen – ' the voice faded, gave out altogether. She saw on her pad: *To my wife, goodbye d –*

The end, goodbye, the end – the words rang on like funeral bells. She began to cry, sitting as she had done before, close up against the radio set. Old Mrs Bishop said with a kind of delight, 'He ought never to have been born. I never wanted him. The coward,' and now Mary Bishop could stand no more of it.

'Oh,' she cried to her mother-in-law across the little overheated over-furnished Crowborough room, 'if only he were a coward, if only he were. But he's a hero, a damned hero, a hero, a hero – ' she cried hopelessly on, feeling the room reel round her, and dimly supposing behind all the pain and horror that one day she would have to feel, like other women, pride.

The Moment of Truth

The near approach of death is like a crime which one is ashamed to confess to friends or fellow workers, and yet there remains a longing to confide in someone – perhaps a stranger in the street. Arthur Burton carried his secret to and fro to the kitchen and back, just as he carried the plates and the orders of the clients, as he had done for years in the Kensington restaurant which was called Chez Auguste. There was nothing French about it except the name and the menu, where the English dishes were given French names, explained at length in English under each title.

Twice in one week an American couple had booked the same table, a small one in a corner under a window, a man of about sixty years and a woman in her late forties – a very happy couple.

There are clients whom one likes at the first encounter and these were among them. They asked Arthur Burton's advice before they ordered and later they expressed their appreciation of his choice. They trusted him even over the wine, and on their second visit, they asked him little questions about himself as though he were a fellow guest whom they were anxious to know better.

'Been here long?' Mr Hogminster asked. (Arthur Burton had learnt his curious name when he telephoned for his reservation.)

'About twenty years,' Burton replied. 'It was a different restaurant when I came called The Queen's.'

'Better in those days?'

Arthur Burton tried to be loyal. 'I wouldn't say better. Simpler. Tastes change.'

'Is he French – your boss?'

'No, sir, but he's been to France a lot, I think.'

'We're happy to have your help. We don't know all these French words in the menu.'

'But it's put in English, sir.'

'I guess we don't understand that sort of English either. Anyway we'll be along again tomorrow. If you let us have the same table – Arthur, isn't it? I think I heard the boss call you Arthur?'

'That's right, sir. I'll see that you have this table.'

'And your help, Arthur,' Mrs Hogminster said.

He was touched by the use of his first name and the smile of real friendship which he received from Mrs Hogminster. In all his years as a waiter, he had known nothing like it before.

Arthur Burton was in the habit of observing the customers superficially, if only to keep an interest in his job which it was too late to change. He was alone in life, so there was no initiative for a change and now he was well aware that it was too late. The crime of death had touched him.

Often when he went home at night – if a bed-sitting-room with a shared shower could be called a home – he would remember certain customers: married customers who seemed to lunch together without interest, watching those who came in with a certain envy if the newcomers had words to say to each other: obvious new lovers who paid attention to no one else: sometimes a married young woman (he always looked at the left hand) with a look of anxiety, accompanied by a much older man. She lowered her voice or even ceased to talk when neighbours took the next table and Arthur Burton wished that he could have left it empty, so that they would be free to solve their problem.

When he got home that night, he thought of Mr and Mrs Hogminster. He wished he had spoken more to them. He felt that he could trust them, like strangers in the street. He might at least have hinted at the crime which separated him from the manager, the cook, the other waiters, the washers-up – only hinted of course, he wouldn't like them to be distressed.

They were half an hour late the next day for their reservation, and the manager wanted him to give up the table to other guests who asked for it. 'They won't be coming,' the manager argued, 'and anyway, there are three other tables to choose from.'

'But they like this table,' Arthur Burton said, 'and I promised they would have it.' He added, 'They are kind good people,' but he probably would have been forced to give way if they had not at that moment arrived.

'Oh, I'm so sorry, Arthur, we are terribly late.' He was touched that she had remembered his name. 'It was the Sales, Arthur. We got involved.'

'*She* got involved,' Mr Hogminster said.

'Oh, it will be your turn tomorrow.'

Arthur told them, 'There are restaurants closer to the men's shops. I can recommend one near Jermyn Street.'

'Oh, but it's Chez Augustine that we love.'

'Chez Auguste,' Mr Hogminster corrected her.

'And Arthur. He chooses so well for us. We don't have to think.'

A man with a secret is a very lonely man, and it was relief to Arthur Burton when he could uncover even a small corner of his secret. He said, 'I'm sorry, ma'am, but tomorrow I won't be here. But I'm sure the manager . . .'

'Not here? *Quelle désastre!* Why?'

'I have to go to hospital.'

'Oh, Arthur, I'm so sorry. What for? Is it serious?'

'A check-up, ma'am.'

'Very wise,' Mr Hogminster said. 'I believe in check-ups.'

'He's had four or is it six.' Mrs Hogminster added, 'I think he enjoys them, but it always worries me. What are they checking you for?'

'They've already done the check-up. Now they have to tell me the result.'

'Oh, I'm sure it will be all right, Arthur.'

'I'm happy you've enjoyed yourselves here, ma'am.'

'We have. All thanks to you.'

Arthur Burton said with truth, 'I'm sorry that we have to say goodbye.'

'Oh no – not yet. We'll be here again on Thursday. Tomorrow, we'll take your advice and eat near the men's shops, but we'll be back the day after to have our last meal at Chez Augustine.'

'Chez Auguste,' Mr Hogminster corrected her again, but she ignored him.

'We are flying to New York on Friday, but we'll certainly see you on Thursday and hear your good news,

(35)

Arthur. I'm sure it will be good news. I'll be thinking of you and crossing my fingers, but I'm sure, quite sure.'

'I have a check-up every six months,' Mr Hogminster said. 'Always satisfactory.'

'Is there anything special you would like on Thursday, ma'am? I can ask the cook . . .'

'No, no. We'll take what you recommend. Until then – and good luck, Arthur.'

Arthur Burton knew that no good luck awaited him. He had known it even before the check-up by the evasiveness of his doctor. He wondered whether a man in the dock could tell the jury's verdict even before they retired from the court in the days when there was still a death sentence: an emanation of shame at what they were going to pronounce. Yet he had a sense of relief because he had at least confessed half his crime to her and she had not rejected him. If, as he believed, the verdict was death, however they wrapped it up in medical phrases of hope, might she be the stranger in the street to whom he could confess the whole? They would never see each other again. She was leaving for New York on Friday. They had no friends in common to whom she could spread the news of his crime. He felt an odd tenderness for her.

That night Arthur Burton dreamt of her. It was not an erotic dream, nor a love dream, a very commonplace dream in which she played an unimportant part and yet he woke with a sense of relaxation he had not known for many months. It was as though he had spoken to her and somehow she had given him words of sympathy which lent him courage to face his enemies, who were about to disclose the shameful truth.

He had taken a day off his work, though his appointment with the surgeon was not until the evening at five, and then he was kept waiting for nearly an hour. The surgeon asked him to sit down in a tone of such grave sympathy that he was able to guess accurately enough the report which followed. 'An operation urgently required ... yes, cancer, but you mustn't be frightened by the sound of a word ... I have known cases as bad as yours ... taken in time there's always a good hope ...'

'When do you want to operate?'

'I would like you to come into hospital tomorrow morning, and I'll operate the next day.'

'If I could come in the afternoon. You see – they are expecting me to be back at work tomorrow morning.' It was not of work he was thinking, but of Mrs Hogminster. She would be expecting news from him.

'I would much rather you had a quiet day in bed. However ... I will be coming to see you with the anaesthetist at six.'

As he lay in bed that night, Arthur Burton thought: doctors and surgeons are not necessarily good psychologists; perhaps, because their interests are so concentrated on the body that they forget the mind, they don't realize how much a tone of voice reveals to the patient. They say 'there's always a good hope', but what the patient hears is 'there is very little hope if any'.

It was not that he was frightened of death. No one could avoid that universal fate, and yet the population of the world was not dominated by fear. All Arthur Burton wanted was to share his knowledge and his secret with a stranger who would not be seriously affected like a wife or a child – he possessed neither – but might with a word of kindly interest share with him this criminal secret – 'I am condemned'. Mrs Hogminster was just such a woman. He had read it in her eyes. Somehow the next day he would find a way of conveying to her the truth, when she asked for the result of the check-up, without words which might involve her husband in his crime. She would ask him: 'What did the doctor say, Arthur?' And his answer? No, no words, a small shrug of the shoulders would be enough to convey, 'It's all up. Thank you for thinking of me,' and the glance that she gave him back would just as discreetly tell him she shared his secret.

He would not go alone into the future.

'You needn't keep that table,' the manager said. 'Those Americans were in yesterday and I found them one they liked much better.'

'They were in yesterday?'

'Yes, they do seem to like this place.'

'I thought they were going to the men's Sales.'

'I wouldn't know about that. I think you talk too much to the customers, Arthur. Often they want to feel alone.'

He left hurriedly to meet Mr and Mrs Hogminster at the door. Mrs Hogminster nodded and smiled at Arthur as they went by to a little table isolated in a corner of the restaurant. They had no view now of the street outside, but perhaps, as the manager had suggested, they preferred privacy, and perhaps too they preferred to be served by the manager himself.

It was only at the end of their meal after they had paid their bill that Mrs Hogminster called to him as he passed to the kitchen. 'Arthur, do come and have a word with us.'

He went willingly with a lightening of the heart.

'Arthur, we missed you, but the manager was so kind and we didn't want to hurt his feelings.'

'I hope you enjoyed your lunch, ma'am.'

'Oh, but we always do at Chez Augustine.'

'Chez Auguste,' Mr Hogminster said.

'With the Sales you were so right to send us to Jermyn Street. My husband bought two pairs of pyjamas and can you believe it, three – three – shirts!'

'She chose them of course,' Mr Hogminster said.

Arthur Burton excused himself and went on into the kitchen. The problem which he had so feared had not arisen, but the thought gave him no relief from the depression of his secret. He was going to say nothing to the manager: the next day he would simply not turn up. The hospital could inform them in due course if he were dead or alive.

He spent as little time as he could in the restaurant, though it pained him to see another waiter looking after the Hogminsters and exchanging words with them.

Half an hour later the manager came into the kitchen and spoke to him. He carried a letter in his hand. He said, 'Mrs Hogminster asked me to give you this. They've left for the airport.'

Arthur Burton put the envelope in his pocket. He felt an immense relief. Of course Mrs Hogminster had done the right thing. They couldn't have talked about his secret in the restaurant for others to hear. Now he would be able to carry with him to the hospital her sympathetic question about his secret and read it again next day immediately before the anaesthetist arrived. He felt alone no longer. He would be holding the hand of a stranger in the street. She could never receive the answer to her question, 'What did the doctor tell you?' but she had asked it in her letter and it was that which counted.

Before putting out the light above his hospital bed, he opened the envelope. He was surprised when three one-pound notes came out first.

Mrs Hogminster wrote: 'Dear Arthur, I felt I must write you a word of thanks before we catch our plane. We have so enjoyed our visits to Chez Augustine and shall certainly return one day. And the Sales, we got such wonderful bargains – you were so right about Jermyn Street.'

The letter was signed Dolly Hogminster.

The Man who Stole the Eiffel Tower

It was not so much the theft of the Eiffel Tower which caused me difficulty; it was putting it back before anyone noticed. The whole affair, though I say it myself, was beautifully organized. You can easily imagine what was entailed – a fleet of outsize lorries to carry the Tower out to one of those quiet flat fields you see on the way to Chantilly. There the Tower could lie quite easily on its side. On the way out, on the misty autumn morning, there had been very little traffic, and what traffic there was I can only describe as humble. No one who tried to pass my hundred and two six-wheeled lorries noticed that they were joined like beads by the chain of the Tower. The private cars would pull out for a moment and attempt to pass, but when the drivers of the Fiats and Renaults saw lorry after lorry stretching ahead they simply gave up and followed the procession. On the other hand I provided a wonderfully clear road for cars coming into Paris: for them the long road from Chantilly was as good as a one-way street. They skimmed by and had no time to notice how the Tower lay over the driving coach of every lorry with no interval between: the Tower went out in a kind of sleeping berth, so many hundred metres long.

I have a great affection for the Tower, and it pleased me to see it, after all those years of war and fog and rain and radar, in repose. The first day it was there I walked around it, occasionally touching a strut: the fourth floor looked a little uncomfortable where it bridged a mild and muddy tributary of the Seine, and I had it eased. Then I drove back to the original site – I was still nervous lest anybody should notice. The great concrete blocks stood there with nothing on them. They were so like tombs that somebody had already left a bunch of flowers addressed to the Heroes of the Resistance. Once a taxi drew up containing the last swallow of tourism alighting there before winging westwards across the Atlantic at the approach of winter. He had a girl with him and he staggered a little in his walk. He bent to look at the flowers and straightened himself with a flush on his well-shaven powdered cheeks.

''Tsa memorial,' he said.

'*Comment?*' asked the taxi-driver.

The girl said, 'Chester, you said we could lunch here.'

'There ain't no Tower,' the man said.

'*Comment?*'

'What I mean to say is,' he explained, waving his arms for emphasis, 'you brought us to the wrong place.' He made an effort. '*Ici n'est pas la Tour Eiffel.*'

'*Qui. Ici.*'

'*Non. Pas du tout. Ici il n'est pas possible de manger.*'

The driver got out and looked around. I felt a little nervous in case he noticed the absence of the Tower, but he got back into the cab and appealed to me sadly. 'They continually change the names of the streets,' he said.

I spoke to him confidentially. 'It's only lunch they want,' I said. 'Take them to the Tour d'Argent.' Quite happily they drove away and that danger was over.

Of course there was always a risk that the employees

might arouse public attention, but I had taken that into account. They were paid by the week, and what man or woman is fool enough to admit that his place of employment has ceased to exist until the week has come round again and the money has been earned? The cafés in the neighbourhood became a great resort for the employees, but no one liked to sit at a table with a fellow-worker in case of awkwardness in conversation. I noticed one uniform cap per *bistro* for an area of a square mile: each man sat contentedly during his hours of duty, drinking a glass of beer or a pastis according to his salary, and rising punctually from his table at the hour for clocking out. I don't think they were even puzzled by the Tower's absence. It could be conveniently forgotten like the income tax. Better not to think about it: if you thought about it somebody might expect you to take action.

The tourists, of course, remained the chief danger. Night fliers assumed a low-lying fog and the Ministry of Air passed to the Foreign Ministry 'for comment' several complaints about radar jamming – a new Russian device in the cold war. But word soon got around among guides and taxi-drivers that when a stranger asked for the Tour Eiffel it was simpler and less complicated to take them to the Tour d'Argent. The management there did not disillusion them, and the view these autumn days was just as good, and they were very happy signing the book at so much a head. I used to drop in and listen to them. 'I got the idea it was more sort of steely,' one of them said. 'I thought you could see through it.' I explained to him how perfectly true that was of the establishment he was in.

A holiday can never go on for ever, and wandering

round of a morning putting a little spit and polish on the struts I concluded that the Tower must go back to work before its employees missed their wages. I could only hope that in the course of time it would find another like myself to give it a spell of country air. I assure him there is little risk involved. No one in Paris could admit that the Tower was absent for five days unnoticed – any more than a lover could admit to himself that he had failed to notice the absence of his mistress.

All the same it was a tricky business, the return of the Tower, and entailed a good deal of traffic diversion. To facilitate this I had laid in, from a theatrical costumier's, uniforms of the police, the Gardes Mobiles, the Gardes Républicaines, and the Académie Française. The diversions included a Poujadiste meeting, an Algerian riot and a funeral oration for an obscure dramatic critic by a friend of mine dressed up as the Minister of Education. I say 'dressed up', but of course there was no necessity for him even to change his name, let alone his face, since no one remembered who this Minister was in M. Mollet's Cabinet.

The tourists had the last word, and curiously enough as I stood at the base of my beloved Tower, which seemed to pirouette into the morning mist, it was the same American arriving in a taxi with the same girl. He took a quick look round and said, ''Tsnot the Eiffel Tower.'

'*Comment?*'

'Oh, Chester,' the girl said, 'where've they taken us now? They never get it right. I'm so *hungry*, Chester. I've just been dreaming of that *Sole Délice* we had.'

I said to the driver, 'It's the Tour d'Argent they want,'

and watched them grind away. The wreath to the Heroes of the Resistance had withered, but I put one dried discoloured flower into my buttonhole and waved my farewell to the Tower. I dared not linger. I might have been tempted to steal it again.

The Lieutenant Died Last

An Unrecorded Victory in 1940

There had been a lot of grumbling in the village of Potter before the astonishing night when the parachutists descended: grumbling about rations, compulsory service, blackouts, all the usual things. Then apparent disaster, a touch of heroism, a good many deaths, put an end to it for a while as it always does, though the hero, old Bill Purves, the poacher, had more reason to grumble than any, for he received no decorations – only a grudging commendation from Major Barlow, the local magistrate who let him off 'this once' with a caution, after he had been caught red-handed with a rabbit in each deep pocket.

You would hardly expect to find Potter the scene of the first invasion of England since French troops landed near Fishguard in the Napoleonic War. It is one of those tiny isolated villages you still find dumped down in deserted corners of what we call in England Metroland – the district where commuters live in tidy villas within easy distances of the railway, on the edge of scrubby commons full of clay pits and gorse and rather withered trees. Walk for three miles in any direction from Potter and you will find cement sidewalks, nurses pushing prams, the evening paper boy, but Potter itself lies off the map – off the motoring map, that is to say. You have to take a turning marked 'No Through Road' and bump heavily towards what looks like a farm gate stuck a mile or more over the shaggy common. Through the gate is nothing but Potter, and Potter is only one public-house, the Black

Boar, landlord Brewitt, one cash store and post office kept by Mrs Margesson, a small tin-roofed church where services are held on the first Sunday in the month, half a dozen cottages, a village pond, and the gates, grounds and mansion of Lord Drew. But even those gates are not used: Lord Drew has other gates on the London road two miles away and never needs to pass through Potter. One of the cottages is inhabited by old Bill Purves: one wall has been repaired with petrol tins and when the door opens smoke blows out into Potter. He is said to sleep on a bed of rags, but nobody but the local policeman has ever visited him there, and the window is obscured by sacking. Three or four times a year – usually on bank holidays – old Bill Purves visits the Black Boar, buys a bottle of whisky and disappears for twenty-four hours. It was suspected, but never known for certain before the parachutists came, that old Purves slipped on those oc-casions into Lord Drew's grounds, laid his traps and lay out all day and night with his bottle – he never seemed to know what cold was, any more than an animal, and he was rather like an animal himself – something grey and fleeting that you see for a moment shambling between hedges. His coat stuck out as if he were a scarecrow on a stick because he carried an old Mauser rifle under his coat, for which he had never paid a licence.

That was the odd scene of the 'invasion', though if you examined Potter carefully you may conclude that it was not an accident that the parachutists landed there. Potter itself could be isolated by a few snips of a wire cutter, and from that little hidden spot in Metroland half a dozen men acting quickly could do an astonishing amount of damage – a mile and a half across unfrequented common and you had the main line to Scotland and the northern coast, and one supposes that the German air chiefs had planned a number of such attempts which our air defences foiled. Their psychological effect might have been incalculable: they would have destroyed the sense of security Englishmen still feel, the security which allows them to grumble. Look at the effect on Potter.

We are a small island and there isn't a village anywhere which isn't accustomed to the sound of aeroplane engines. The plane they heard in the Black Boar was flying fairly low – perhaps 3,000 feet, but there was nothing out of the ordinary in that.

It was the fag-end of a cloudy spring day. Mrs Margesson in the cash stores had just closed the post office counter because it was 6.30; the shop remained open for general goods till 8.00, and the lean man who was Lord Drew's undergardener was criticizing the beer in the public bar. 'It's the war they tell you,' he said bitterly. 'Everything's the war.' There wasn't a man left in any of the cottages; they were all in the public bar except old Purves, and the women were washing up the supper things.

Old Purves with his coat sticking queerly out and a bottle of whisky in his deep poacher's pocket was skirmishing along by Lord Drew's wall among the high nettles. The gamekeeper had sworn to get him and he wasn't taking any chances. He was the only one to see the parachutists descend.

He looked up under his old grey brows with a kind of angry astonishment as a number of men suddenly appeared in mid-air under things like enormous parasols.

He didn't know what they were; he only had a feeling they were best avoided. 'It didn't seem right,' he said afterwards; he meant that it didn't seem fair, people peeping at you like that out of the sky. That was all he saw for a long time because just at that moment he found the weak point in Lord Drew's wall. The men were in uniform – for their own protection, one supposes; otherwise they would have been liable to the death penalty as non-combatants, but their uniforms caused no immediate astonishment in Potter, because we are so used in these days to uniforms: what with AFS and ARP and all the other initial letters we are prepared for any uniform, even a German uniform. Mrs Brewitt saw them at work on the telegraph and telephone wires and thought they were something to do with the post office. Only her son, who was sixteen and, alas! for him, knowledgeable, said they were Germans. 'Nonsense!' Mrs Brewitt said.

Mrs Margesson in the cash stores hardly looked up when the officer came in. He carried a large-scale map of the district and had a revolver at his belt. His steel helmet made her think, 'manoeuvres'. She said promptly, 'The post office is closed,' because she didn't think he looked like a shop customer. He said, 'Madam', and that struck her as foreign: a Frenchman or a Pole, she thought: he was a young man, very fair, and his uniform was very muddy; he sounded nervous and preoccupied. She smiled. 'Yes. What can I do for you?'

'Please,' he said, 'go at once to the inn.'

'The inn?'

'Yes. You must go at once. Everyone must go.'

'I don't understand.'

He said with embarrassment as though he were making a rather absurd claim, 'I am a German officer and this village is occupied by my men.'

With great presence of mind Mrs Margesson picked up the shop telephone and dialled a police call. The young man made no attempt to stop her. She could at once tell why – the wires had been cut. At that moment through the window she saw Driver, the village constable, being impelled down the road towards the Black Boar by two men in uniform; he had probably been digging in his garden as he was in his shirt sleeves.

More or less the same scene took place all over the village. Everybody who was not already at the Black Boar was rounded up and persuaded, pushed or even carried there. The Germans were determined that nobody should leave the village and carry the alarm, but they missed young Brewitt who had hidden in the outside lavatory and, of course, old Purves.

The German officer addressed them in the public bar. He told them that nobody was in danger from him or his men; all they had to do was keep quiet. The gamekeeper, who had been caught hunting old Purves and had a black eye, said in a loud voice, 'It's a scandal.' The German officer paid him no attention. He went on to warn them that any attempt to escape would be fatal; he said frankly, 'Our chance depends on none of you getting away,' and that reference to a chance – for what chance had a dozen Germans planked down in the middle of England? – suggests that they had a desperate hope they might be picked up again by plane before their presence was discovered. He said, 'You will be closely guarded and any attempt to escape will mean death.' He added with a note of entreaty, 'You've only to remain quiet for a few hours.'

All this time, of course, old Purves had been comfortably curled up just inside Lord Drew's wall. He knew that the house was shut up and the only possible interference would be the gamekeeper or the policeman. The policeman was digging and would be too tired later to prowl: as for the gamekeeper old Purves despised him. He set a couple of traps, loaded his gun, opened the bottle of whisky and began to drink: he always calculated that a little drink improved his aim, and he had high hopes of a bird or two that evening. He was disturbed by a shot: his first feeling was indignation rather than curiosity. Lord Drew was away: a shot meant a rival poacher. He took another long drink, hid the bottle where he could find it again in a hole in the clay bank, and then peeped over the broken stones of the wall. To his astonishment he saw young Brewitt running and zigzagging down the road that led out of the village to the gate and afterwards to the main road.

What had happened was this. Young Brewitt, who had a romantic mind, remained convinced that what he had seen was actually a party of German soldiers cutting the telephone wires. He even guessed how they had arrived. The romantic mind found no difficulty in the idea. So he hid. He would probably have remained hidden if one of the Germans who had a tidy soul hadn't wanted to visit the lavatory. He pulled open the door and young Brewitt darted out like a rat; the soldier was taken by surprise and let him get a start. He shouted and young Brewitt ran the faster: other soldiers ran out of the inn and one of them fired and missed. It suddenly became very essential to get him. Three men waited with their guns raised until he should reach the gate.

So to his amazement old Purves watched the astonishing behaviour of young Brewitt. The boy leapt and zigzagged down the road; then he came to the gate and scrabbled desperately at the catch; three rifles went off together and young Brewitt fell. 'The bloody Bojers,' Purves said aloud, the old brain creaking rustily back forty years to South Africa and an ambush on the veldt.

Young Brewitt wasn't dead: they had fired, humanely, at his legs; but he was crippled for life. He shared with Purves the heroic events of that evening, but there were always some who said that he had intended to hide all night in the lavatory. About old Purves's movements and intentions there was no doubt at all.

He first of all unearthed the whisky bottle, took a long drink and hid it again; then he had a look at his traps and then he sidled like a ferret out of Lord Drew's grounds into the high nettles. He slid among them crouching, his chin protected by a two weeks' beard: he had got his gun out from under his coat – the old Mauser rifle that went back like his memory forty years to another war; it was as if 1914 to 1918 were an interlude he had hardly noticed at all.

Young Brewitt had been carried back into the Black Boar and two men had been left on guard. The rest with the lieutenant now set off across the common towards the railway line, carrying picks and crowbars, their rifles slung; two carried a box between them. Old Purves work-

ing his way, like a 'bloody Bojer' himself, from gorse bush
to gorse bush, followed. The sun was setting over by
Fenham Heath station three miles away; it shone just
over the curve of the horizon on the last prams going
home, on the circulating library where the Vicar's wife
was changing her detective story, and on the little stream
of commuters back from town, carrying attaché cases.
That was a quiet, orderly, conventional world to which
neither old Purves nor his quarry belonged: they were
united out of sight but hardly out of hearing in a common
spirit of wildness, vindictiveness, adventure. Old Purves
gave an odd little chuckle as he bobbed quickly out of
sight behind a gorse bush.

He knew the common, of course, as well as he knew
Lord Drew's estate, and at first he thought, because of
the tools they carried, which he could now see clearly in
the darkening air, that they were bound for the gravel
pit, dry and abandoned twenty years ago, a hundred
yards from the railway line. A miniature one-track line
connected it with a disused siding, and an old steel truck
lay on its side, tipped off the rail. But the Bojers passed
that by, clambering up the embankment on to the line
beyond. Old Purves, worming his way along towards the
gravel pit, thought they were a beautiful sight, outlined
like that against the sky. They had left their rifles, all but
two men, in the bushes below the embankment, so that
they could slide quickly and inconspicuously down if a
train appeared – on that long stretch of rail you could see
an engine's steam two miles away. Now four of them bent
and pulled and worked at the rails, two followed the
lieutenant further down the line with the box, and two

stood rather slackly on guard, watching the empty waste of common and the up and down line.

They never saw old Purves get down into the gravel pit. He scrabbled up to the edge, where a bush hid him, and got a line on one of the armed guards – the unarmed ones could wait. With a man's body clear against the sight, old Purves chuckled. It was like youth again: all sorts of sly memories came back, of nurses at Pretoria and drinking evenings in Jo'burg. He pulled the trigger and before the shattering explosion of the ancient rifle could clear, the man was down, holding his stomach with both hands: his rifle toppled over the embankment and rolled.

It was like one of those trick films that suddenly stop and then go on again, fast. Down the line the officer had swung round with his revolver out: the two men with him had their mouths open. Picks and crowbars suddenly stopped: one of them in mid-air. Then life started again. The guard fired at old Purves's smoke and the bullet kicked gravel up against his cheek: the men working dropped their tools and tumbled down the embankment to where they had left their rifles. Old Purves chose his next victim.

The Germans were shockingly out of luck. The bright sunset was behind the poacher, dazzling their eyes: he had their silhouettes lit up like dummies in a shooting booth. He began to suck excitedly through a gap in his teeth and fired again. A man half-way down the embankment tumbled, but old Purves had given away his position and though he ducked at once, the guard, stretched out now on top of the embankment, nipped a bullet close by his ear. When he took another peep the workmen had got their rifles, though the two men with the box a hundred yards up the line were all unarmed. That meant that four rifles could be brought to bear, not counting the lieutenant who was crawling back. Old Purves chuckled again: it was more fun than rabbit shooting.

But the others too had learnt their lesson: the lieutenant was shouting orders which the poacher couldn't understand. While the guard remained on top of the embankment the others, taking advantage of the bushes, began to circle round to get the sun behind them. Old Purves wasn't disturbed: he knew his battlefield. From one end of the gravel pit ran a trench, but because of the overhanging bushes it couldn't be seen from above: to the watcher on the embankment he was cornered. Old Purves, ducking under the gorse into the little hot tunnel, jolted away, looking more than ever like an earth animal going to ground. The trench sloped gently up and soon he was on all fours, then out he came into the tall bracken. He took a daring look: the guard had his eye fixed on the gravel pit: the two men up the line had left their box and were crawling towards their rifles: the three men and the lieutenant had made a half circle and were now steadily creeping towards the pit – their backs were half turned to him, and again they had the worst of the light.

Old Purves at this point of the game could have retired safely, with all the honours, but he was enjoying himself. He never liked to leave good game alone even if it meant risking capture. He waited until one of the men, in screening himself from the supposed enemy in the gravel pit, had exposed himself to his enemy in the flank – then old Purves let him have it 'proper', or rather he meant to: for the first time he nearly missed altogether: the man dropped his rifle, slumped heavily down nursing his hand. 'Goldarn it,' he said and ducked at once under the bracken.

Not one of the men suspected that the shot had come from the rear. They were almost at the rim of the pit now: the lieutenant gave an order: they leapt to their feet and were over it. But this time old Purves couldn't have made a mistake if he'd tried – firing quickly he got two: only the lieutenant leapt to safety.

By that time the two unarmed men had reached their rifles and the guard had spotted old Purves. Before he could get down a shot from the embankment got his left shoulder. He sat still among the bracken and wished he had some whisky with him. He tried to move, but the swaying bracken gave him away and a bullet missed him by a centimetre. He swore softly: this time the bloody Bojers *had* trapped him and there were still four of them left.

He was saved by a goods engine from Fenham Heath: it was going north with a string of empty trucks. The three men now hugged the ground under the embankment and a whistle warned the lieutenant to keep out of sight. They didn't want a warning carried up the line: they couldn't tell that the nearest troops were twenty miles away at least.

As the engine came into sight old Purves saw his chance. He bolted through the bracken towards the overturned truck which would protect him from all of them but the lieutenant – the lieutenant only had a revolver and the light now was shockingly bad. Nobody fired at him. Then he swung round and sent a shot at the officer who had got out of the gravel pit, but the pain in his shoulder was upsetting his aim and he missed.

All the same, though he didn't know it then, he'd won the game. They were scared and harried and didn't know what to think: all the lieutenant was concerned with now was to get his business finished quickly. He dodged round to his men and they all began a kind of strategic retirement up the line, along the edge of the embankment: old Purves sent another shot after them, ineffectively. Then he swore gently because he'd only got one shot left.

He watched the four men, a little puzzled. They were climbing up on to the embankment again: he didn't shoot because the light was bad now and his eye was out. One man fired a warning shot at him which nicked a tiny piece off the edge of the truck. The others were opening the box: it seemed to contain string . . . Old Purves was irritated: he didn't like being ignored. He took aim rather wildly and fired.

For a moment it was as if the end of the world had come, blasting up against the truck which sheltered him: there were lamentable cries. When the fury of air and fire had died away, he came out of shelter and picked his way through the bushes – there was nobody left to fire at him. This was massacre.

He didn't like it: it turned his stomach over like dyna-miting fish: the strange thing was that the rails were the only things left untorn.

The lieutenant was not dead: he called out in English,

'Kill me. Please kill me.' Old Purves always felt pity for broken animals, but he hadn't a bullet left. Then he saw the officer's revolver three yards away . . . Afterwards he looked through his pockets: there was nothing of value, but a photograph of a naked baby on a hearthrug again made his stomach turn over.

That was really the end of old Purves's battle: the rest was only what they call 'mopping up'. He went back to his traps and drank what was left of his whisky: two rabbits had already been snared. Then with the rabbits in his poacher's pockets and the lieutenant's revolver in his hand he went down cautiously to the Black Boar. There they had listened fearfully to the sound of the shots and the explosion: the guards were nearly as scared as the people of Potter. When old Purves appeared suddenly behind them with the revolver they surrendered at once. They, with two wounded men among the gorse, were the only survivors of the only parachute descent – it had been a discouraging failure for the German High Command because of old Purves's absence from the village, in Lord Drew's grounds. Driver, immediately he was released and saw the rabbits, charged him with poaching and as I have said, a week later he was released with a caution and a rather cold commendation. He was quite gratified: he didn't expect medals and as he said, 'I've got one back on them bloody Bojers.' For a while people visited him and gave him tips in return for history – 'They runned just like little rabbits,' he used to say – and for the sight of a few souvenirs, but that source of income soon failed, and he was back in no time on the wrong side of Lord Drew's wall. One souvenir he never showed to anyone – the photograph of the baby on the mat. Sometimes he took it out of a drawer and looked at it himself – uneasily. It made him – for no reason that *he* could understand – feel bad.

A Branch of the Service

I have been forced reluctantly to retire from a profession which I found of great interest and on a few occasions even dangerous because I have lost my appetite for food. Nowadays I can eat only in order to drink a little – before my meal a glass or two of vodka, and then a half bottle of wine: I find it quite impossible to face a menu, leave alone the heavy three- or even four-course meals in restaurants which my profession demanded.

I owed it to my father that I got the job I am now leaving, though he died before I was, as we call it, re-cruited. My earliest memories are the smells of a kitchen – they are happy memories even though I now find it a burden to eat. The kitchen was not one in my home: it was, as it were, an abstract kitchen which represented all the kitchens in which my father cooked – kitchens in England, Switzerland, Germany, Italy, and once I believe for a short while in Russia. He was a great chef – but he was never officially recognized. He moved from country to country. He was never out of a job, but he never kept a job long because he always knew better than his employer when it was time for him to leave.

Of my mother I remember nothing – I think she must always have been left behind on our travels. How I enjoyed eating in those days, yet I never learnt how to cook. That was my father's pride and secret. What I learnt were languages – never very well but a smattering of many. I could understand better than I spoke. The man who later recruited me understood that. I remember him saying, 'To understand is the only important thing. We don't want you to talk.'

You may wonder why it was necessary for me to eat large meals in order to keep my job. Even in a good restaurant one does not feel bound to eat more than two courses and one may always linger a long time over the wine. Yes, but I was supposed to be judging the food not the wine, even awarding stars to the food in the fashion of Michelin, but of course stars differently designed. I even had to inspect the lavatories.

In my father's eyes I would never have made a first-class cook, and he didn't wish me to spend my life as a kitchen help. Through an admirer of his English cooking in a little restaurant in St Albans where he worked for a year before quarrelling with his employer, he introduced me to a new organization which called itself International Reliable Restaurants Association, but before I had finished my first six months' training they changed the name. IRRA was a little putting off because of the Irish difficulties, and so they became instead the International Guide to Good Restaurants or the IGGR.

Their advertisements and their reputation rose together; at any rate for English customers, for they soon outbid Michelin. Michelin was too nationalist. Michelin awarded to Paris in those days five stars to eight restaurants, while to London they gave no five stars and only two four stars. The IGGR was far more generous, and that proved an advantage.

I had been an inspector for the IGGR for two years before I was recruited for special duties.

As I learnt during my training in these so-called duties we were not really interested in the number of stars or even in the cleanness of the lavatories. The people with whom we were concerned were unlikely to be found in very expensive restaurants, for costly eating can make the eater conspicuous.

'Rich eaters are not the main interest of this section,' my instructor told me, 'here we look out for an ordinary customer. Especially those who are more than usually ordinary – they are the likely ones.'

I found his lessons at first a little obscure, until he told me a story which explained one of my puzzling memories of Paris. He said, 'Of course in this section we are not concerned with police work, but all the same we have taken a hint from the French police. Do you remember the lottery sellers who used to come into the bistros and the small restaurants in France?'

'Yes. You never see them now.'

'And yet lottery selling is not illegal. They are gone because they had outlived their usefulness.'

'What was their usefulness?'

'The police showed them the photographs of wanted men – small fry, thieves and the like, and they would go from table to table looking at the faces. This gave us an idea for a rather more important work, a work which involves our ears more than our eyes.'

He made a long pause; he meant I think to arouse our curiosity, and curious we certainly were at having been taken away from tasting food and inspecting lavatories.

(62)

But we were wrong. There was a gleam of amusement in our speaker's eyes. 'The lavatories are of particular importance,' he said.

'From the point of view of cleanness of course?' a novice (not me) asked.

I still had no idea what our instructor was talking about. 'No, no,' he said. 'Cleanness isn't our concern, but the lavatory is a private place if you want to exchange a word or a packet with a friend. Unless of course your friend is a woman, but we'll come to that possibility later.'

A lot of other possibilities came later.

'There are phrases in conversation that you hear in a restaurant which are worth attention. *Pas de problème* is less interesting in France where it is in such common use, but if one of your neighbours in a small unfashionable restaurant in Manchester (a restaurant which hasn't got even one star) says, "There's no problem" it's worth paying attention.'

I think that he felt among the novices a certain scepticism. He went on, 'A hundred chances to one, of course, nothing of interest – of obvious interest – will follow – but make a note. There remains the one chance. The lavatory too – though perhaps the chances there are a little greater. For example two men peeing beside each other and talking. Our organization fills a gap – an important gap in security. A house is watched – but that again is not our job. The telephone is tapped. Not our job. Even street meetings are in other hands. But restaurants – we are doing a great service to the state.'

A question came to my mind. 'But when once we have

given a star to a restaurant we have no excuse to go on eating there?'

'You are wrong. Two stars might be gained for the next edition – or a star could be lost. A certain blackmail is sometimes necessary. You will always be welcome and given the best food.'

The best food – yes, that was my problem. A career of eating. Of course it didn't worry me at the beginning, and what attracted me was not so much being of service to the state as the hint of mystery about the whole affair. The phrase 'no problem' stayed like a tune in my ears.

2

Of course, when first sent on duty one made serious mistakes, but unlike other professions one was excused – even sometimes praised – for a mistake because it might have added a little to one's experience. My first bad mistake – which in any other profession would have ruined my career – happened to be concerned with a lavatory. But I would prefer to speak of my first lucky success which far outweighed my lavatory error, although that success too concerned a lavatory. The occasion took place in a three-starred restaurant, a smart one, but not too smart like the Ritz. In my first three years I was only told to take a watch in the Ritz once, the expense was too great and the chances too small. Waiters there were apt to notice strangers. I had been shown a photograph, but a very bad one, of a suspect who apparently had been seen at this restaurant more than once and was believed to be a foreigner. In his case they had already paid three experienced watchers – one a day – and they were almost ready to give up. His companion at table was always different.

Quite by chance – in our profession nearly everything is a chance – I happened to be sitting at the next table to a solitary man. Some instinct had made me choose the table next to him for I could see little resemblance to photographs I had been shown. However there was a foreign look about him, and perhaps (I might have imagined it) a look of impatience or anxiety, and his table was laid for two. He had ordered a glass of port (not a usual aperitif for an Englishman) and he lingered over it. I lingered too over my very dry Martini, trying to outlinger him.

At last the friend he was awaiting arrived – a woman. I write 'friend', but the greeting which he gave her struck me as very odd – 'Pleased to meet you', that very anti-quated English phrase, was spoken in a distinctly foreign accent.

For the rest of my meal there could no longer be any malingering. In my training I had been taught that I must always finish my meal and pay my bill while those whom I had chosen to watch were still eating. Of course I could spend quite a lot of time, after paying, with a coffee, but I must be prepared to leave my table a little before those I watched or a very little after. I had to keep in touch, at all costs, but avoid the suspicion of keeping them under observation.

This early experience of mine in the Royalty restaurant was a physically very painful one, for the pair whom I had chosen to watch had a large meal and I have always, as I have said, had a very small appetite. First they chose a mixed salad, then roast beef, then cheese and then to my horror, they ordered a dessert – this too was a foreign touch for in England we finish with cheese. It confirmed for me that the two were of different nationalities, and that 'pleased to meet you' had been an agreed signal. A momentary disagreement over cheese before dessert confirmed me in thinking that the man was French and the woman English.

Their conversation was mainly on the subject of Flaubert about whom the woman was writing a book. Of course it occurred to me that Flaubert might be the pseudonym of a third agent and Madame Bovary of yet another. They made no attempt to lower their voices.

'It's very good of you to see me,' the woman told him. 'I have used your great work on Flaubert a good deal, and it's very kind of you to allow me to quote from it.'

I knew little of Flaubert's life, but I began to learn quite a lot, and there really seemed nothing wrong with the couple.

'I'd have liked to see you once again and show you my text before it goes to the publisher, but I know how busy you are,' the woman said.

'Yes, I would like to see it, but I'm afraid I'm off by an early plane tomorrow. At 9.30.'

I made a mental note to check the time and destination, but I had really lost all suspicion and I would have called it a wasted day if it had not been for the cigarettes. After the meat course, when they were waiting for the cheese trolley, she offered him a cigarette.

He hesitated, and I thought he glanced at me.

'A Benson and Hedges Extra Mild,' she told him.

(66)

'Yes, I do like one of those, but do you mind – I only smoke one after I have finished eating. It's a habit.' However she took a cigarette and laid it by his plate.

'You don't mind if I smoke?' she asked.

'Of course not.'

He lit her cigarette and the cheese trolley arrived. She chose a Stilton and he chose a Brie. I chose the smallest bit of Gruyère that I could persuade the waiter to cut and shuddered at the thought of the dessert which was yet to come. I took an ice and after the apple tarts which they picked the woman took a coffee. I did the same. He seemed to have forgotten her cigarette, for he left it still unlit beside his plate. Perhaps a Benson and Hedges, I thought, was too mild for his taste. They continued to talk about Flaubert, but what they said was quite beyond me. At last the man asked for his bill and I quickly did the same, but theirs came first and I had no time to wait for it before I followed them from the restaurant. The man still carried his cigarette. Perhaps he had no intention of smoking it, but didn't wish to offend his companion by throwing it away.

At the door he said goodbye to her. She said, 'We haven't spoken at all of *Education Sentimentale*. If you could manage another meeting . . .'

'I'll certainly do my best,' he said. 'It has been a great pleasure meeting you.' When she had left he turned away towards the lavatory still carrying his cigarette. A tidy man, I thought, he's going to throw it into the toilet, but all the same a reasonless curiosity had settled in my brain. There was another reason too. I wanted to practise my new profession. A good cook progresses through his

(67)

errors. A short pause and then I followed him walking as quietly as I could.

He was washing his hands when I entered and he had laid the cigarette to one side out of the way of the water – that eternal unsmoked cigarette. I snatched it and before he had time to turn I was out of the lavatory. There was no shout from behind me – only the sound of pursuing feet. At the hotel entrance I pushed the porter to one side and ran into the street. Luck was with me. A taxi had just deposited a customer. As I drove away I saw the customer rushing after me into the street followed by the waiter who was waving my unpaid bill. Poor man. I paid it later indirectly with interest by recommending the restaurant for a fourth star, which it certainly did not deserve.

In the taxi I looked more closely at the cigarette. There was an odd feeling in the centre – a kind of hardening of the tobacco, and at one end a kind of roughening in the packing of the cigarette. I was careful not to finger it more. It had already passed through three hands and was a little damp from its lavatory lodging – there seemed reason enough for all this. All the same I had learnt in my training to hand over any object however trivial belonging to a suspect, and this I did as soon as I reached the office of the International Guide to Good Restaurants. Then I sat down to write my report, and my instinct made me enclose with it the untidy cigarette.

3

I hadn't given in my report long when the telephone sounded. 'Scramble,' my chief's voice said, and I touched the button which would make our conversation unintelligible to anyone who might be tapping our line.

'The woman I feel pretty sure was English and the man French, I think, but they spoke to each other in English although they were both experts on Flaubert.'

'I think they wanted you to listen. They were proving, you might say, their innocence.'

'But are they guilty?'

'Guilty as hell. You've done a first-rate job. Come along in an hour and see me.'

When I went to him the cigarette lay torn in half on his desk in a small litter of flakes. 'Benson and Hedges Special Mild,' he said with a smile of satisfaction. 'Low in tar content, but certainly not low in valuable information.' He showed a little bit of wrinkled paper. 'A good way to conceal it,' he said, 'in the middle of a cigarette.'

'What's on it?' I asked.

'We'll soon know. Microdots and a code of course. You've done a good job. It was very acute of you to take the cigarette.'

Such a good job indeed that they forgave me several months later for a very bad mistake which also involved a lavatory.

4

The cigarette had led us to a new suspect for our file, a doctor who had connections with the chemical industry. He was now placed under continuous surveillance; a whole team of us was employed night and day. His open practice was in a small country town not far from the factory which used him as a consultant when one of the employees went sick. He had been very thoroughly vetted by MI5, but our relations were closer to MI6 and there was a good deal of rivalry and even jealousy between the two establishments. The foundation of the international food guide was regarded by MI5 as an intrusion into their territory, and it was true that we had not passed on to them the information contained in the cigarette. Counter-espionage abroad certainly belonged to MI6, but our food guide was international and it would be inefficient to split the English section from the foreign. No watcher was employed more than once in two weeks and always at different mealtimes in order that the suspect would never become aware of a familiar face. Unfortunately for me the doctor was a man of inordinate appetite and after two months my turn came at the hour of dinner – the hour when his appetite was greatest. Unfortunately too I had suffered from a succession of heavy meals earlier. To award a star even to breakfasts had to be considered, and it was extraordinary how many people still preserved a pre-war appetite for what is still called an English breakfast as distinct from a continental one – eggs and bacon, or even worse sausages and bacon, sometimes even preceded by a helping of haddock.

I took over from his watcher outside a quite simple inn which was called the Star and Garter only half a mile from his own house. We were the only diners and I sat down at a table well away from his. I noticed he looked quite often at his watch, but he was obviously not expecting a friend for he had already chosen his meal. To my horror when I looked at the menu I found a set menu at a very reasonable price and he had ordered the first course which was an onion soup and my stomach cannot abide onions. If I left out the soup I would find myself well in advance of him and I would be out of touch with him when I finished the last course. Another watcher was stationed in sight of the door who would take over when he left, but I had to remain till then in sight of the doctor in case he was contacted during his meal. A doctor was always of course liable to a phone call when he was away from home, but the Star and Garter telephone would have been tapped as soon as we knew where he was in the habit of dining.

I allowed myself a glance at him every now and then when he lowered his eyes to the obnoxious soup. To me he looked a thoroughly honest man. Why would an honest man be mixed up with the man of the cigarette? Then I remembered he was a doctor. A doctor doesn't judge his patients. If he had attended the deathbed of a murderer that wouldn't have made him a murderer. If a priest appeared on our microdot file would he be reasonably a guilty man? The doctor finished his soup and ordered roast beef. Reluctantly I did the same. I had to keep in step, though I could already feel the effect of the onion soup. He was a slow eater and read a newspaper between bites. I was glad that he showed no interest in me. It confirmed my impression of his honesty. It was a cold night and I felt sorry for the watcher outside keeping his unnecessary vigil.

To my distress the doctor ordered an apple tart to follow. The only alternative on the little restaurant's menu was an ice-cream, but an ice-cream needs to be eaten with some speed before it melts, so I was forced to order the tart. My trouble was I suffer from acidity, and when the doctor followed the tart with a piece of cheese, I had to leave the table, for I felt the approach of diarrhoea. The lavatory was upstairs and as I left I ordered my bill, so as to be ready to leave on my return if the doctor didn't wait for coffee. If I found him with coffee I could spin out the time with a little difficulty over change and when he left my colleague would take over. 'And see him safely home to bed,' I thought with irritation at this unnecessary routine watch.

I won't go into the unsavoury details of my diarrhoea – it was a severe one and more than five minutes had passed before I went downstairs to the restaurant. I found that the doctor had gone, and I thought with relief, 'My job is over.' I would take something to ease my stomach when I got home.

As I paid my bill I remarked to the waiter, an elderly man, who, I found, was also the landlord, 'Not much custom tonight.'

'At night,' he told me, 'the bar trade's better. And we do more at lunchtime – passing motorists, but the doctor's a good regular and he likes simple food.'

I felt it my duty to inquire a little more about our suspect.

'Doesn't he ever dine at home?'

'No, he's a single man.'

'Not much custom for a doctor in a place this size?'

'There's always the flu. And babies. But of course his main work is up at the chemical factory. Two hundred men. Plenty of patients there. I hope you enjoyed your food, sir, and that we'll see you again. It's a small place but my own, and I keep a sharp eye on the kitchen.'

'I can tell that. Here is my card.'

'International Good Food Guide! My goodness! I never expected to see one of your fellows in my little place. So that's why you went to the lavatory?'

'Yes. We always inspect those. And I looked in on the kitchen on my way,' I lied. 'I could tell at a glance . . .'

'What?'

'Clean. Which I already knew from the food it would be.'

'It's very kind of you, sir. I do hope you'll come again.'

'Not for a year. In the meanwhile we'll give you a mention in the guide.'

'I'm very honoured, sir. Perhaps some of the big shots from the factory will read it.'

'What I advise you in the meantime is to have at least two menus. Perhaps then we could promote you to a star.'

'Never did I dream . . . When I tell the missus . . .'

'By the way what do they do in the factory?'

'All sorts of medicines, sir. Even cures for the hiccups they say. Me, I am content with a bit of Eno's. It serves most purposes.'

I bade him a warm goodbye and gave him a copy of the guide in which his restaurant would appear in the next edition. I was glad to be off because my stomach was still queasy and I had no further duties that day. I would go home and perhaps as the man had reminded me take a glass of Eno's.

I went outside and to my astonishment saw my fellow watcher pretending interest in a shop window across the road. He turned and saw me with equal astonishment.

'What the hell have you come out for?'

'What are you doing here?'

'Waiting for the doctor of course.'

'But the doctor's gone.'

'He hasn't passed that door.'

'Oh the hell. There must be a back door.'

'But why didn't you signal me as soon as you lost touch?'

'I had to go to the loo. I was only gone a few minutes and he wasn't there when I came down. He came in this way and I thought he'd gone out the same way and you'd be following him.'

'He must have had suspicions.'

'I took him for an honest man whatever the damned microdots said.'

'We've certainly messed things up this time.'

5

That was exactly what my boss said when I reported to him. 'You've badly messed things. You should never have left the restaurant before him. Even for a minute.'

'It was the onion soup and the tomatoes.'

'Onion soup and tomatoes! Is that what I have to tell the big chief?'

'I had diarrhoea. I couldn't stay and shit in my trousers.'

'You know I would have sacked you like a shot, if you hadn't made that splendid coup with the cigarette.'

'You needn't sack me. I resign. But I'd swear – microdot or not – that man was honest. He was no traitor.'

'Traitor is a silly word that journalists use. A traitor can be as honest as you or me. That chemical factory has connection with chemical warfare. A man can feel that chemical warfare is a betrayal of the world we have to live in. He could be fighting for something greater than his country. An honest spy is the most dangerous. He is not spying for money, he's spying for a cause. Look, that cigarette is more important than this mistake. One learns from mistakes, and you are a good learner. You have given me a good idea of how to use your mistake. He may have been suspicious of you. Or it may have been his regular drill. To go in by the front and go out by the back.'

I said, 'I can't go on. I'm sorry. I can't go on.'

'But why? This mistake of yours will be forgiven and forgotten.'

'But the onion soup. Tomatoes. And all the meat I have to eat. Garlic with the lamb. Cheese as well as dessert. Why do all these suspects have such a good appetite?'

'Perhaps it gives them time to observe the people around them.'

'But *they* never seem to get diarrhoea.'

'About your diarrhoea. I have an idea.' He paused and played with his pencil. 'Suppose we gave you a week's holiday.'

'I don't need a holiday except from onion soup, and tomatoes etc.'

'But I see a way of using them. Suppose you stayed a week at that little hotel and had all your meals there. The doctor would begin to accept you as a regular. You would consult him about your stomach. He might give you a treatment. Of course you would take nothing he gave you, for if he remained suspicious he might try to poison you. Any prescription he gave you would send on to us and we would have it examined. If there was anything dangerous about it our suspicions would be confirmed and we would close in on him.'

'And if they weren't?'

'We'd give him more time. He would need to have *his* suspicions confirmed too if he's a man with scruples. We would think of some way. A warning from somewhere would reach him. Or one of your own reports perhaps. We would watch his reactions very closely. All you would need to do is . . .'

'To eat,' I said. 'No. I've made up my mind. I can't make a career out of eating. No more onion soup, no more tomatoes, no more garlic. I resign.'

So it was that I abandoned the International Guide to Good Restaurants. Sometimes from curiosity I buy a copy of the latest number. At least I have done one good deed in my life. The little country restaurant remains as a 'mention' in the guide, though it has never received a star.

An Old Man's Memory

I am writing in 1995 and old people's memories are short. Small wars come and go, even the deaths in Gaza and Beirut which caused such a stir in the eighties seem to belong to history now, but I doubt whether the year 1994 will ever cease to horrify me. The event of that year has a quality of nightmare about it – deaths in the darkness, in the depths of the sea, deaths by mutilation and drowning. The rotting bodies of the unrecognizable rise occasionally to the surface even today on both sides of the Channel.

Elaborate celebrations were prepared for the opening of the Channel Tunnel and the first two trains were arranged to pass each other in mid-Channel. There had been some dissensions in England, of course, just as there had been in the Paris celebrations of the Revolution in 1989, because of the devastation of the countryside in Kent by the new autoroutes between Dover and London, but the dissidents were few when the first cross-Channel train from Paris arrived in Dover. Mrs Thatcher, who had won her fourth electoral contest, was of course there on the platform to greet the French train as it came up from the sea and halted at Dover to join in the celebration. The French Ambassador was present and for some obscure reason Mrs Thatcher was accompanied by the Minister of Defence. Perhaps it was to reassure a few of the dissidents who remembered the failure of Hitler's plans to invade England after our flight from Dunkirk. If the Tunnel had existed then, would there have been time to destroy it and if it had been destroyed would we have rebuilt it when the war was over?

In 1994 all was well prepared. I wasn't at Dover myself. It was easier to watch the whole affair (or so I believed) on television. As the French train emerged from the Tunnel the 'Marseillaise' was played and afterwards 'Rule, Britannia!', but not 'God save the Queen'. Perhaps the Queen shared some of her people's doubts, but Mrs Thatcher stood up very straight and played the part of Britannia. On the other side of the Channel the President of France waited to greet the British train, but it never arrived. The news reached us just as Mrs Thatcher began her well-prepared speech. Bombs had exploded under the Channel and the British train had been destroyed before it reached Calais with the loss of all lives.

Who were the terrorists?

It was believed that Semtex was the explosive used. In the case of an air disaster in the eighties when a plane had crashed over a village in Scotland it had only needed a radio cassette player to hold three hundred grammes of Semtex. There had been great advances since then, and explosives could be timed now for days not hours in advance. The new explosions went off soon after the British engine passed the half-way line under the Channel. The IRA was of course the prime suspect, because of its activities in Germany and its relations with Gadaffi who was known to have supplied the IRA with Semtex, but the Iranians had never forgiven England for its support of Rushdie nor the Americans for having shot down their innocent airliner. As it happened there were even more Americans on board the train than English.

Who had known where to plant the bombs? For four years hundreds of workmen had been employed in

constructing the Tunnel. It had been like an open challenge to the terrorists to do their worst. Of all these
hundreds it must have been easy enough to find one or
two who were ready, in return for large sums of money,
to sketch plans of their work in the Tunnel and, the best
spots once chosen, to find others to plant cassettes.

Much publicity had been given in the Press to the
security measures for which those involved in construc-
tion were not ultimately responsible. All luggage had been
X-rayed, every passenger passing through the same sort
of arch as we have in our airports had been meticulously
checked. But had all appropriate measures been taken in
the depths of the Channel itself?

The terrorists were in no hurry. They had plenty of
time, four years of time, to plan, to choose, to corrupt.

Two years have passed now and there have been no arrests, but what may surprise even the terrorists is that the
Euro-Tunnel Company, encouraged by shareholders and
aided by the British and French Governments, has an-
nounced that the Tunnel is to be reopened and work has
already begun and should be finished by 1997. The costs
will be almost as great as building the first Tunnel.

I have spoken of the shortness of an old man's memory,
but I wonder if anyone's memory will be short enough in
1997 to persuade a passenger to climb on board the
carriage which will take him down into the depths of the
Channel, as dimly lit as the great Tunnel under the Alps,
but with water and not rock above, and how many corpses
still rotting below the rails?

The Lottery Ticket

Mr Thriplow bought his first and last lottery ticket in Vera Cruz. He had had two glasses of tequila to give himself the courage to board the awful little hundred-ton Mexican barge with an auxiliary engine which was the only method of getting to the small tropical state he wanted to visit. He felt himself, as he took the very first sheath of tickets the small girl offered him, driven by fate – perhaps he was. I don't often believe in fate, but when I do I picture it as just such a malicious and humorous personality as would choose, out of all people in the world, Mr Thriplow to fulfil its absurd and august purposes.

Then, as far as concerned an aunt in London and a female cousin in Brisbane, with whom he used to keep up an animated and whimsical correspondence, silence descended on Mr Thriplow. One or two events in that obscure state crept into the News in Brief on the foreign page of *The Times* – an assassination, for instance, which the aunt noted and then told her friends, without conviction, 'Henry must be having quite an exciting time.' He was, but you didn't associate Henry Thriplow with excitement.

About forty-two years old and a very well-to-do bachelor, Thriplow was a timid man, but his timidity took a curious form, for it drove him, whenever he had a holiday abroad, into discomforts you didn't connect with timidity. He couldn't bear social contacts, and so he chose for the scene of his escape those parts of the world where his fellow-tourists didn't congregate. He went, the year I'm writing of, to Mexico, but he didn't go to Mexico City, or Taxco or Cuernavaca or even Oaxaca, although his aunt urged him to look out for a decorated serape and he knew his Australian cousin would value some silver ear-rings. Instead – he gave as his rational excuse that he wanted to investigate the career of Cortes – he chose a grim little tropical state, where there was nothing at all to see but marsh, mosquitoes, banana plantations and a public gaol which probably *did* go back to Cortes.

You came after forty hours by sea, wallowing in almost intolerable discomfort in a boat lit only by oil-lamps in the bow and stern (when the captain wrote his log a sailor stood by with an electric torch), you came in sickness and stench and the weariness induced by the wooden shelf they called a bunk, to the River and the Port. There you lay another day against the bank propped up with the carcasses of old ships, the mosquitoes drilling round like sewing machines. There were a few wooden huts, one little dusty plaza with a statue of Obregon, the buzzards rustled overhead, and out beyond the river the fins of sharks glided by like the periscopes of a fleet of sub-marines.

Ten hours up the river between the banana plantations lay the capital. Thriplow's ship went ashore twice on the way: the fireflies flickered like a city on either bank, and the oil-lamps gave an effect of curious melodrama to the shapes of the coconut palms and the banana trees. Then round a bend came the real lights of the capital looking sophisticated and important and surprising in that wild obstinate region.

It was false, of course, that effect of sophistication:

Thriplow had no need to fear the shrill bargaining tones of American women hunting for serapes: there was nothing in that town to attract anyone – except Thriplow. The barge was tied up to a mud-bank, and Thriplow went ashore over a plank thrust across twelve feet of green sour river: a policeman took his suitcase and shook it, listening for the surge and clank of contraband liquor (spirits were prohibited), and a kindly spectator switched on an electric torch to save him from sliding back into the water.

There was only one possible hotel and after Thriplow had left his suitcase, he walked up into the plaza to see what life there was. All that there was existed there. Some sort of an election was on, he couldn't tell what: red stars and the words Popular Frente decorated all the walls, and round and round the plaza in the deep sour heat the younger people walked – the men one way, the girls another. A blind man in his best white suit and his best straw hat was led by a friend: it was like a religious ceremony, going on and on in all-but-silence, in front of a dentist's (the hideous chair lit up like a wax figure in the window), the Federal Prison with white colonial pillars and an armed soldier and a press of dark faces at the bars, the Treasury, the Presidencia, the Syndicate of Workers and Peasants, and a few private houses where behind the unshuttered windows old ladies swung back and forth and children sat on hard straight bought-by-the-dozen Victorian chairs.

Thriplow could speak very little Spanish: he had a phrase book for his vital needs: and he had little hope that in this blistered and comfortless town there would be anyone at all who spoke English. Sitting nervously up in bed, watching a cockchafer bang against the high ceiling of his great bare room and the ants troop up through the tiles, Thriplow could feel that his object had already been achieved – he could look back on Kensington and his aunt's house and his regular comfortable routine with real nostalgia; he could return – unlike the regular tourist – filled with a passionate sense of the beauty of his own home.

Breakfast next day in the only restaurant; a stroll through the market above which the buzzards hovered with black serrated wings and tiny idiot heads: lunch in the same place: an uneasy sleep upon his bed, a walk up to the plaza, supper, a glass of mineral water to clean his teeth with (Thriplow was careful of his health), and bed again. It wasn't much of a day – there wasn't even a church he could examine (they had been destroyed throughout the state and the priests hunted out), in which he could watch with his faint disapproval the Roman ritual and the native superstition. As for the lottery ticket – he had forgotten that completely.

It came back to his mind at lunch-time on the third day, when a man approached his table with tickets. He asked to see the old list, and there, framed in the centre of the long columns, was his own number, 20375. His first – and last – lottery ticket had won 50,000 pesos – about £2,500 in English money. The flies revolved round the ugly beef on his plate, and a beggar – an Indian with little wisps of hair on the chin and lip – stood just inside the doorway watching the lunchers (he never spoke a word, probably knew no Spanish, he was like the figure in a morality play to remind the well-fed of the hungry).

Mr Thriplow's immediate sensation was shame – he felt like a foreign exploiter, a gringo. He had spent 5 pesos on the ticket: what right had he to all this money? The lottery seller told everybody in the room about it, and they all had to see his ticket and the list and they all told him what he had to do – he understood the word 'banco' all right. As he left the restaurant he tried to salve his conscience a little: he emptied his notecase which held 50 pesos into the Indian's hand. The man showed no pleasure: he moved quickly away, as if he didn't know what God might do next.

The news had reached the bank long before Thriplow arrived there. Smug and sleek and smiling, the half-caste manager came out to greet Thriplow, sweating under the armpits. He had almost as little English as Thriplow had Spanish, but Thriplow could guess from the wide gesture that he was putting the poor resources of the bank at his disposal. It was almost as if the news had reached the vultures too, for they came rustling down across the roofs and settled in the road with their hideous little heads peering this way and that for a death.

Thriplow sat on a hard shiny rocking-chair and listened to the manager. He could only understand a word here and there, as the hot day drooped above them. It sounded as if investments were being discussed: apparently he couldn't take the money out of Mexico. He said, suddenly, petulantly, the heat was getting him down, 'I don't want the money, I don't need the money. This place needs it more than I do,' and was startled to see the immediate comprehension in the manager's brown half-breed eyes.

'You are,' the manager said, 'a benefector,' as if he

were making a statement and not asking a question.

'I don't need your money,' Thriplow repeated. He smoothed his pale hair nervously, afraid that he might sound theatrical. 'I should like to do good – for this country.' It was really an enormous sum for a Mexican state so poor as this – he pictured himself with gentle satisfaction as a kind of Carnegie. 'A library perhaps.'

'A benefactor,' the manager said again. All the English words he knew had Latin roots – the result was rather like a tongue-tied Dr Johnson. He picked up a straw hat and said, 'Depart.'

'Where to?'

The man was vague. He said something about the Presidencia. Thriplow let himself drift with fate – and haven't I described fate already as humorous? He drifted – after the absurd straw hat, full of holes like a sieve – up into the plaza, into a waiting-room in the Presidencia. It appeared that his benevolence was to be arranged by the Governor himself – free library, Thriplow wondered, a hospital, a scientific institute, perhaps a debating society? Or alms houses. There were long conversations on the telephone. A man like the traditional bandit in tight trousers with a highly decorated revolver holster watched him – with malevolent good humour over a red scarf.

'The Governor is absent,' the manager said. 'Again we depart,' and he led the way back across the plaza followed by the bandit. He headed for a door marked Dentista and flashed explanatory gold teeth. 'Pain,' he said with satisfaction, 'pain.' They went right in – to the room with the chair and the drill. The sun was reflected from a whitewashed wall back into the room blindingly. The

Governor sat in the chair, his mouth plugged open with cotton wool, and a buzzard stalked across the yard like a domestic turkey, looking for offal.

The bank manager explained rapidly in Spanish, and the Governor listened, tipped back in the chair with his mouth open. He was small and fat and middle-aged with a blue chin and a good-humoured boyish expression. The dentist changed a needle and a look of agonized apprehension crossed the Governor's face: he gestured imploringly towards the manager as much as to say, 'Go on talking. Go on. For heaven's sake.'

The manager stopped dramatically with an emphatic sentence: Thriplow had understood nothing. The Governor was almost horizontal: his feet were on a level with the manager's mouth: he tried to heave himself up and nodded violently, dislodging a piece of cotton wool.

Then the dentist swung the drill over and the Governor's face was again convulsed – boyishly. 'Pain,' the manager said. 'Pain. We depart.'

They came out again into the little steamy plaza: a few people sat under the trees drinking gaseous fruit drinks – chemical pinks and yellows. A man came down the steps of the Presidencia, his revolver holster creaking dryly in the stifling day, and a little squad of soldiers went by, small men, Indians, with slovenly olive uniforms and rifles slung anyhow. 'Education,' Thriplow thought, 'that's what these people need,' and his heart swelled happily with a sense of benevolence and power: his old Liberal traditions stirred: one of his ancestors had had a statue erected to him in a foreign land.

The bank manager turned this time away from the

bank, away from the Presidencia. He trotted across the square, very hot, very intense, mopping his forehead. The force of his momentum carried Mr Thriplow with him. He was aware of nothing but that little steaming back making for the office of the Workers' and Peasants' Syndicate – nothing but that and a girl who moved away at their approach. It wasn't any beauty which caught Thriplow's attention – there were many girls in this town with better features and Thriplow in any case cared nothing for women – it was a curious lost inimical air she had. She wore her clothes as if they didn't fit. 'Who's that?' he said. She watched him from the centre of the plaza with suspicion.

'Religious,' the manager said, as if that explained anything at all, bobbing through a whitewashed door into a little dry patio. The patio contained a number of packing-cases filled with bottles of mineral water, a dead fountain and some shrivelled flowers, an empty sardine tin.

'Interpretation,' the manager said. He began to talk animatedly in Spanish with someone Thriplow couldn't see through a door. And then the oddest figure of that odd day emerged – a very fat man with curly hair and a jolly face. He was dressed in dirty white drill stretched to bursting round his thighs and he carried a billiard cue: his belt shone with bullets and a heavy holster rattled against his side. He waved the cue cheerfully at Thriplow. He said, 'I speak English – very fine. I am the Chief of Police in this – ' he smiled idiomatically, 'lousy hole.' Somebody struck a billiard ball, and the Chief of Police peered with anxiety into the room.

He said, 'You can't trust them. They are not – sports.'

He turned again to Thriplow and went rapidly on: 'This man wants me to tell you the Governor is made very happy by your present.'

'And what,' Thriplow said, 'does he propose to do with it?'

'Progress,' the Chief of Police said. 'We are very backward here.' Again he started at the click of a billiard ball.

'A new school?'

'All in good time,' the Chief said. 'First we must defeat reaction.'

'Reaction?'

'You have heard of the election?'

'I don't want the money used for politics,' Thriplow said.

'Politics, no, no. But this is not politics. Rebellion. They are plotting rebellion. They are getting arms from Germany, Italy, Japan. They are selling Mexico.' He gestured out at the little hot plaza, the fruit drink stalls. 'If they win, it is reaction. The Church comes back, the bishop.' He paused impressively. 'The Inquisition.'

'Oh, surely not,' Mr Thriplow protested.

'Yes, the Inquisition.'

'But I wouldn't like to feel,' Thriplow said, 'that this money . . . well, you know, I am a foreigner . . . I don't want to add to the political bitterness.'

'You will be loved,' the Chief of Police said. 'Your money will be . . . sinking fund . . . for progress. Just give your ticket to this man.' He peered anxiously through the door, and then struck with an idea turned floridly back. 'The gratitude of the State . . . a Statue, or perhaps a drinking fountain, but there is no spring . . . a seat of marble in the plaza with *your* name . . . what is your name, señor?'

'Thriplow.'

'An inscription. From all friends of progress in the State in honour of their foreign benefactor.'

'It's very good of you.'

'Not at all. Where would you like the seat, Señor Tipno? In front of the Syndicate? Or by the Presidencia? Under that tree? We will clear out the fruit-seller.'

'It is really too good of you.'

There was nothing to do at night. The electric dynamo on the ground floor of the hotel buzzed and droned, and in the hotel itself, on the first floor, the lights flickered and the beetles banged on the walls. They came swarming up from the riverside in droves: the floor crept with them. The proprietor and Mr Thriplow sat on wicker chairs swinging back and forth in the thick hot air. After a while the proprietor found a few words of English, a few words of French: a doubtful communication of ideas was set up between him and Thriplow. Somewhere, a long way off, in the direction of the plaza, there was a lot of noise and shouting. 'Election,' the proprietor explained, fanning himself with a Mexico City paper four days old. A boat hooted on the river.

The proprietor began to complain – a dreary lament for the good old days. As far as Thriplow could make out, in the days of Porfirio Diaz they had had a Governor who had died a poor man – it had never happened since. Mr Thriplow tentatively produced the words, 'Reaction . . . Inquisition.'

The proprietor suddenly discovered a phrase: 'Now,' he said, 'we die ... *comme les chiens.*' Why should a man not have a priest at his deathbed ... if he wanted it? It might be superstition, but when had a man a better right to superstition than when he was dying? He lapsed gloomily into silence, hitting out at the beetles with his paper.

'But the wealth of the Church,' Thriplow protested. The proprietor didn't get his meaning. '*Iglesia ...*' Thriplow said. '*L'argent ... mucho dinero.*' A hollow laugh was his reply. The noise from the plaza went on and on.

Thriplow said, 'After all it is a democracy here ... You have a vote. If you want reaction, you can vote for it.' He went on a long while explaining democracy to the hotel-keeper: every now and then a word seemed to penetrate – 'ballot' for instance. Suddenly the old man gave tongue. It was confusing and a little disturbing. Thriplow felt that he had probably not understood correctly. The word 'lottery ticket' came in, and once Thriplow was convinced that he had been called a fool. The idea that Thriplow got – it was probably an inaccurate one – was this: the Governor's position, in spite of the police and the federal troops and the trade union, was shaky. It was incredible, but it had really seemed that he might lose the election. Because the wages of the police and the soldiers had not been paid for months. The word 'gold teeth' came in, but that could hardly have been the Governor's only extravagance. His opponent had been placarding the town with accusations – and the police had not torn down the notices. But now tonight everybody had been paid – in full – because of the lottery ticket.

Mr Thriplow tried to suggest in English and French that the victory of progress ought not to be endangered by the loss of a few weeks' wages.

The proprietor suddenly and unexpectedly lost his temper – the noise now was so great that he shouted at Mr Thriplow. 'Progress.' The electric light went out completely, and then went on again showing the proprietor's face convulsed. He screamed, '*Pistoleros. Asesinos.*' There was some cheering in the street outside.

Thriplow went out on to the balcony. A platoon of soldiers was going by: they were a little drunk – you could tell it in their broken and stumbling march – but it was not they who were making the noise. Four women, some children and about eight men were screaming themselves hoarse behind the soldiers: with mechanical fervour, 'Viva, Viva, Viva.' People watched them from doorways, taking no part: the soldiers marched unsteadily between the dark river and the silent watchers, little bemused Indian faces, rifles slung, marched close together like untouchables.

'What are they doing?' Thriplow said. The proprietor replied that they were probably going for the other candidate – to arrest him. This time Thriplow felt sure he understood because he had guessed the answer.

'Why?'

The proprietor laughed with despairing amusement and replied, to make sure, in French and Spanish. '*Trahison, defamacion*,' and in English, 'Who will care?'

'Where does he live?' The soldiers were marching slowly.

The proprietor told Thriplow. Thriplow ran down the stairs, treading on the beetles: as he reached the ground floor, he looked back, and then the light went out again: the old man in the wicker chair at the head of the stairs was whisked into darkness in the middle of a swing – it was like an expression of indifference.

If the soldiers were really on their way to the house and not to their barracks, they were soon outdistanced, and the house was easy to find. Thriplow knocked, and the door came open at once, as if somebody had been waiting, with anxiety, for just such a message. Thriplow passed through into a tiny patio. A woman said, in English, 'What do you want?' It was a very poor place – a lamp on a table exposed one small room like a cell. Thriplow said, 'Where's the candidate?'

'My father has gone,' the woman said.

He looked at her for the first time: it was the girl he had seen in the plaza. She recognized him accusingly. 'You were with the Chief of Police.'

He said, 'They are coming to arrest him.' He began to explain that he abhorred their politics, but he felt a certain responsibility, because of his lottery ticket. He had been hasty.

She said, 'It doesn't matter.' Her calm relieved him: he thought perhaps he had been making a mountain out of a molehill. He saw sewing on the table and remarked, 'I do embroidery too.'

'One has to live.'

'You speak English very well.' It was like a social call.

'Of course,' she said. 'I was educated there.'

'You don't think we need worry your father?'

'He knows,' she said, 'all there is to know.' She watched him with immense reserve.

He had a sense of anticlimax in the little poor patio. He said, 'If I've been the cause of any inconvenience, I must apologize.'

'It was you who gave the money, wasn't it?'

'It was, but you understand . . . no personal feeling. I am a Liberal. I cannot help sympathizing with . . . progress.'

'Oh, yes.'

'I detest Fascism. I cannot understand how a patriot – I am sure your father is a patriot – could take arms from Germany, Italy . . .'

'What a lot you believe,' she said with faint derision. He took another covert look round the patio – the rooms had nothing but the barest needs of life – a table, a chair, a bed hard and unpromising. He felt a kind of fanaticism even in the furniture. He said with distaste, 'You live very frugally.'

'We are very poor,' she said.

A crucifix hung on a wall above an Indian bed, just a raised piece of mud floor covered with a straw mat. He said uneasily, 'They told me you were religious.'

She corrected him, 'A religious. I was in a convent, but they destroyed it. It was where the cement playground is, by the river, and the swings.' She made a mild movement towards the crucifix. 'That is treason. They will probably come and search. They will want all the excuses they can find.'

'But I can't believe . . . now that I see you here . . . that your father is in any real danger.'

(93)

'He's in none. They are in danger . . . and you.'

Thriplow was startled. He said: 'You mean the reactionaries? They may start trouble?'

For the second time that night somebody lost temper with Mr Thriplow. She flared suddenly out at him: 'The stupid names you use.' She dropped her voice and said, 'I am sorry. Of course you are English. Poor man, what a fool they've made of you.'

Thriplow was shaken with irritation. He tried to break free of the whole absurd tangle. 'Well, I'm glad your father's safe.'

She said, 'I have not been fair to you. You *should* know. They arrested him half an hour ago. You may have seen the soldiers going back to barracks. They had to fill them with liquor first.'

'Then why did you say . . .' He stopped. He knew why. She was breaking the news to him as if it was *his* father. You owed that to the man responsible. He read the whole story in her dry pitying eyes.

She said, 'You've heard of the law of flight. Of course they never really run away . . .'

Mr Thriplow had no words at all, but somewhere at the back of his mind hate began to stir – hate of the lottery seller, hate of the bank manager, the Governor, the Chief of Police, even of the dead victim of his imprudence, hate of all who had so unexpectedly broken into his life, hate of the new ideas, the new words. Hate increased its boundaries in his heart like an annexing army.

The girl said gently: 'If you liked to give me some money . . . I have none in the house . . . you would feel then perhaps – not so bad about it. You would have done your best for us. You could go home quite happy. You are a good man.' She had the kind of copybook psychological sense you often find in nuns. He took out his pocket-book and gave her everything he had. The action dictated by hate was like an action of love. She said: 'It is more than I need – but perhaps I can bribe someone and get a priest to bury him – from another state. Here, you see, we die like dogs. Thank you.' She was determined to make the affair easy for him. She was abominably aloof on the height of her religious resignation, watching poor devils, like beetles, making their mistakes. She said, 'I can see you are a kind man. Only ignorant . . . of life, I mean,' she added with the devastating pride and simplicity of the convent.

Mr Thriplow went out into the street: he thought of his cousin in Brisbane and his aunt in Kensington: a sour smell poured up from the river, and a beetle struck his cheek and detonated off through the electric night. He heard it strike a wall. Somebody somewhere sang in very simple Spanish – a melancholy song about a rose in a field, and hate spread across Mr Thriplow's Liberal consciousness, ignoring boundaries. He heard the bank manager saying, 'Pain. Pain.' Individuals dropped and shrivelled in the enormous conflagration of his inter-necine war: he didn't even know the candidate's name. It seemed to Mr Thriplow, treading in his disappointed exile beside the sour river, that it was the whole condition of human life that he had begun to hate. A phrase came back to him out of his childhood about one who had so loved the world, and leaning against a wall Mr Thriplow wept. A passer-by, mistaking him for a fellow-countryman, addressed him in Spanish.

The New House

Mr Josephs offered Handry a cigar with the air of a curator showing a choice exhibit, but the architect brushed it aside, and tenderly unfolded his plans upon the table. Then he waited in a kind of awe for the first exclamation of pleasure.

Mr Josephs, however, stood by the fender and carefully cut his cigar. He was in no hurry; he had never in his life been in a hurry.

'Nice little patch of ground I've got,' he said airily, and waved his hand to express the sense of size, 'near on a thousand acres.

'I like hills, with a bit of wood on them; park, as you might say. It gives one kind of space. One can build with a – a gesture. That's the word, gesture.' He put his hands behind his back and took a long puff. 'I shall wake up this countryside. It's too sleepy by half. You are a lucky man, Handry, and you've got a big chance. I'll make you rich, Handry, rich enough to clear out of this village and start in London. I like you, old son, I like you.'

Samuel Josephs suddenly noticed the architect's face, the pallor, and the brightness of the eyes. He fetched out a glass and a bottle of port, for no one could deny that the great Josephs was a kindly man. 'Have a drink, Handry. You've been overworking.'

Handry's hand shook as he took the glass and drained it, and a small drop fell upon the blotting paper by his side. It spread like a blotch of blood on a dead man's shirt front.

'I'm grateful, sir,' he said, 'very grateful. I've been in

this place close on thirty years. When I started I used to dream of something like this, and I always had that stretch of land in mind. I've measured and worked out every yard of it, and twenty years I've spent on the plan, cutting out and putting in, and altering this and altering that. Every moment of time, between putting up cottages for the folk here, has gone to it. So you see I'm pretty grateful, sir. It means a lot to me.'

'Why, Handry,' said Mr Josephs with that expensive smile, so well known to newspaper readers, 'you're an interesting man; bit of a poet, eh? And this,' he looked anxiously at the lengthening ash, 'is what they call your *magnum opus*. The Bard says something about that, I'm sure, but I can't remember it. Quotations more in your line, I expect.'

'I don't care much for poetry, sir, I'm afraid,' returned the architect. 'It's too immaterial. I prefer land, mortar, bricks; things I can shape and feel.'

'You're wrong, Handry. Take my word for it, you're wrong. I've made my pile and I'm proud of it, but I made it by Vision, Handry, Vision. The motto of all my papers was "Follow the Light". Materialism will never get any-where; compared with vision it's unsaleable. Ever read Longfellow? No? You should. That's the man for my money. He gets there every time. I took something of his for my Topical News:

> O thou sculptor, painter, poet!
> Take this lesson to thy heart:
> That is best which lyeth nearest;
> Shape from that thy work of art.

(98)

Cute, eh? Well, now let's see your work of art, Handry, old man.'

With trembling fingers, Handry held down the covers of his plan, and tried to look on it with the eyes of a stranger. Yes, no one could fail to see its beauty, the delicate, retiring lines, like a shy woman. It would melt into the trees as his own dream into reality. He waited in nervous, blushing expectancy, like a mother showing her first baby to the outer world.

But the praise did not come. There was a long and dreadful silence, and Handry, watching his employer's face, could see his mind searching for some kind remark. Josephs cleared his throat and at last it came. 'Very clever, Handry, I'm sure. Very clever. But not exactly what I want. I want something a bit bigger in conception, something that can be seen for miles around. A landmark, Handry.'

The architect's deadened silence caught his attention, and he gave him another of his well-known, comforting smiles. 'I don't say, Handry, your drawing hasn't got its points. It has. But you haven't had the practice, old man. Everything you've done has been on too small a scale, and naturally you've been getting into rather a groove. I don't despair of you. With help you are going to knock me up something really good.'

'I suppose,' said Handry wearily, 'you want a Van-brugh.' He rolled up his plans, and stood up. 'Well, there's no more to be said.' He held out his hand. 'Thanks for giving me a trial, Mr Josephs.'

'Don't be a fool, man,' cried Samuel Josephs sharply. 'I like you, and I'm going to have you. I only want you to work out something a little more noticeable, in white stone with Corinthian pillars. It will take you very little time to make a rough sketch, which we can go over together.'

'It'll take me a very little time, will it?' cried Handry. His face was white again, but his eyes were leaden. 'It's taken me twenty years to finish this plan, and you say it has points. Do you think I'll be the instrument for spoiling this land? You can take the dirty job to your friends in London,' and he turned on his heel.

'Now, Handry, Handry, my dear fellow,' Mr Josephs was quite perturbed, 'don't forget your vision. This is petty, Handry, petty. I offer you five thousand pounds to build me a house. You should remember your client's wishes before your own. To be frank, your plans are quite hopeless, quite hopeless, Handry.'

'Curse you, you fool,' muttered the architect between clenched teeth, holding back a childish outburst of tears.

'Are you going to throw away all that money, my dear fellow, just for stupid pride? Anyway, consult your wife before you come to any rash decision. You can't afford such feelings, Handry. Besides, which of us, I wonder, is the true artist. There is no such thing as idle show, Handry. What says the bard?

> Nothing useless is or low;
>> Each thing in its place is best;
> And what seems but idle show,
>> Strengthens and supports the rest.

'The light, Handry, don't forget the light.'
But Handry had left the room, had dashed into the

road, as though from an evil spell, and yet he knew that all this struggle was vain. He was trapped, held fast by the ropes that bind all, his wife, his family, the world. Soon he would come slinking back, mouthing embarrassed apologies, to perpetrate the betrayal.

The bicyclist smiled bitterly at his companion. 'Isn't it a monstrosity?' he cried. 'This used to be one of the most beautiful views in the country. That fellow Josephs's philanthropy goes too far. His architect was a fellow in the village here, with no more views on art than the average rustic. And the abomination is a waste, for Josephs never lives in it, never comes near it.'

'Good evening,' said the strange little man, who had been standing close by, also regarding the house upon the hill. He was an elderly man, with pathetic, puzzled eyes, and he carried an umbrella. 'You are looking at the house?' he asked. 'It is rather fine, I think, don't you? It is so imposing, and such a landmark. It can be seen for miles, positively, for miles. Once I disliked it, but I had queer ideas in those days. There was a plan . . . Yes, my ideas were queer, very queer. I have a better appreciation now, I think. Do you read Longfellow? You should. He has very inspiriting ideas. I did not always think so, but there, one changes.'

A light gleamed suddenly in his eyes, and he drew himself up proudly. 'I am Handry, you know. The Architect,' he said vaguely, and, umbrella upon arm, sloped away into the shadows.

Work Not in Progress

My Girl in Gaiters

As old age closes down one is frequently asked to tell a story to 'the little ones' – grand-nephews and grand-nieces and the like. 'You write books. You must be able to tell a story.' And yet the ignoble truth is that my ideas for future novels are seldom quite suitable. On these occasions I have to fall back on the musical comedy I have planned for years – a fairy story surely innocent enough for the innocents, but even then I sometimes lose a parent's trust. The name I have given it is *My Girl in Gaiters*.

When the curtain rises twelve bishops of varying ages dressed in gaiters and wearing those curious black hats with little strings attached used by the Anglican church are standing on the stage. They sing the opening chorus. During the first verse a young man comes on to the stage at the side. You can recognize he is a JOURNALIST *by his notebook and pencil. He listens to the bishops, who sing a song roughly on these lines*

> Thirteen bishops for convocation,
> > Gaitered bishops and true,

We've come to give you our authorization
   For the prayers to be offered by you.
We have given consent to Our Father
   In spite of its Roman tone;
We have set our seal on a Grace for a meal
   If free from a gluttonous moan.

But we've kept very wary of any Hail Mary
   In spite of the High Church vote,
For we are much too Broad to admit any fraud
   Across the Lambeth moat.

Thirteen bishops for convocation . . .

JOURNALIST [*interrupting*]:

   You counted Bath and Wells as two,
     And if you count again,
   You'll find there are only twelve of you.
     Explain, Your Grace, explain.

   The bishops look at each other in consternation and begin to count again.
   The explanation of this mysterious occurrence is that one of them has been kidnapped, and soon all will be involved in the same fate. A gang of thugs in London have decided to kidnap the whole of Convocation, in the hope of laying their hands on the chasubles belonging to the Church of England. They are ill-educated men and have mistaken the word chasuble for the word chalice. The twelve thugs are led by a woman who is the brains of the gang (and the only woman in the cast). When I

have had an extra glass of champagne I dream that she is played by Vivien Leigh.

The kidnapping of the bishops proves successful and they are locked without their trousers in the cellars of a derelict building belonging to the Ecclesiastical Commission. The thugs then draw lots for who plays who. The ringleader naturally is *ex officio* Archbishop of Canterbury – the first time since Pope Joan that a woman has occupied so high an ecclesiastical post. Unfortunately for the false bishops the Bishop of Melbourne has arrived in London to act as an observer at Convocation. The various stages at which his suspicion is aroused I have yet to work out. They include a country Confirmation where the bishop performing the rite mutters some highly unecclesiastical words when he finds too much hair oil on one boy's head. The Bishop of Melbourne sets himself to track down the offenders.

He penetrates to the heart of the conspiracy at Canterbury where he meets the false Archbishop. There in the rose garden strange feelings of love puzzle and disturb him. The false Archbishop too falls in love with the Bishop of Melbourne and her conscience is stirred. At the end of the second Act she confesses all to the Bishop. In horror he decides to leave England for ever, but his love is too great to turn her over to the police. At the end of the second Act the Bishop of Melbourne is sitting at one side of the stage beside a telephone and the Archbishop of Canterbury, the false Archbishop of Canterbury of course, is sitting at the other side also by a telephone. The Bishop begins with a sad reminiscence of the past.

WORK NOT IN PROGRESS

BISHOP OF MELBOURNE:

There was a maid at Wallyhoo
With whom I saw my first sunrise.
There was a deaconess at Starving Camp
Who made me blush and close my eyes.
But my girl in gaiters,
Oh, my girl in gaiters,
She has tricks like Walter Pater's
With her Mona Lisa eyes
All the secrets of the sea,
Every kind of ecstasy,
And when she wants to speak to me
She lifts the telephone.

FALSE ARCHBISHOP OF CANTERBURY:

Melbourne, Melbourne,
Cantuar calling.
Stop your stalling,
Drop your moral tone.
There's a heart beneath a cassock,
And a knee upon a hassock,
A motor ride from Dover,
So come right over,
But come alone, damn you, come alone.

BISHOP OF MELBOURNE:

Cantuar, Cantuar,
Melbourne calling,
Can't hear a word you say,
Oh, how faint you are.

[*The two in duet*:]

CANTERBURY:

Melbourne, Melbourne,
Cantuar calling,
Stop your stalling,
Drop your moral tone.

MELBOURNE:

Cantuar, Cantuar,
Melbourne calling.
Can't hear a word you say
Oh, how faint you are.

ARCHBISHOP OF CANTERBURY:

It's your girl in gaiters,
Melbourne, Melbourne,
All the tricks of Walter Pater's
With my Mona Lisa eyes.

BISHOP OF MELBOURNE:

And the damn'dest kind of lies.

[*The* BISHOP *slams down the telephone.*]

CURTAIN of Second Act

(The second act of a musical comedy in my youth always ended in self-sacrifice or misunderstanding.)

Alas! the rest of the musical has not yet been very fully

(106)

worked out except for the escape of the real bishops from their prison, while the false bishops are on their way to Convocation. The false bishops are hurrying down on to the stage between the stalls. The little ribbons in their hats are now wireless aerials through which they are 'Calling all cars,' 'Calling all cars.' In Convocation the Bishop of Melbourne turns up unexpectedly. The false bishops realize they have been betrayed and round on the Archbishop of Canterbury. She is defended by the Bishop of Melbourne until the arrival of the true bishops in their underclothes routs the impostors.

All is well again between the lovers and they sing a melodious duet. (I am anxious that the charm of the old melodies should be revived in my musical.)

HE:

In my very first parish
A dream I used to cherish
Of a girl in a scarlet gown,
And in the quiet scenery
Of my very Rural Deanery
I decided her name was Brown.

As a very young archdeacon
Very early I'd awaken
And wonder if my dream was Sue.

SHE:

But, oh, what a shock!
Instead of a frock
There's a girl in gaiters for you.

HE:

There's nothing could be lighter
Than my bishop's buckram mitre
When laid in the scales against love.

SHE:

Add a golden chalice
And a moated palace?

HE:

They'd still kick the beam above.
Oh, I'd gladly abdicate
To a country curate,
If you'd be the curate's wife.

SHE:

What, hurt feelings in the choir
And collections for the spire,
For the rest of a humdrum life?

HE:

When Matins were over,
How dotingly I'd hover

SHE:

Above the 'little stranger' in the pram?

HE:

When the Guilds got up a dance
I'd be sitting in a trance

SHE:

Wending home with me at midnight in a tram?

HE:

Oh, I hate the Visitations
And the endless Confirmations
And the lonely nights I spend.

SHE:

But if I cannot marry
Because of Dick or Harry – ?

HE:

I'm tired of being celibate,
I'll gladly be expatriate
With a loving female friend.

In the last scene the Bishop of Melbourne is returning to Australia up the gangplank of a liner and the former false Archbishop of Canterbury accompanies him. She no longer wears a shovel hat and black gaiters, but a little top hat and scarlet gaiters, and the theme song of the thugs is sung for the last time as the curtain falls. The song was written many years ago by my brother, when Controller of Overseas Services (BBC, not ecclesiastical), and I cannot quite remember the words. It is called 'Top Hats in Hell', and begins:

In hell they all wear top hats,
Top hats in hell.

Perhaps that is the one unsuitable song for the young, but then I didn't write it.

Murder for the Wrong Reason

The low brief cry could have reached but a very little distance into the night from the open window of the room, and perhaps, before he died, Mr Hubert Collinson may have realized that it was hopeless to expect any reply.

A long, tortuous dream is said to last but a few seconds of time as we record it, and in the short interval that elapsed between the moment when the unexpected knife slipped into his breast and the moment when his heart ceased to beat, Mr Collinson may have heard his cry reflected as a faint, tingling echo from the glass of his bookcase and the glass of his door and the glass of the mirror that had hung on the wall for so many years, to be used by his female clients.

And yet the sound did find an audience, for half a minute later a heavy knocking began at the door and a voice called, 'Collinson!' When there was no reply, the man outside put his shoulder to the locked door and burst it open. He gave a hurried glance at the body, which was curled in an attitude of obsequious humility in a swivel chair, and took off his soft hat, not in any reverence for the dead, but because it was a close night.

His glance at the body seemed perfunctory and without pity, a professional acceptance of the fact of death. He leant out of the window and blew a whistle several times, until he received his answer, shrilled from several quarters of the night at once, as though a host of invisible playgoers were competing for a taxi. The sense of this hidden wakefulness in an apparently sleeping world for a moment disturbed his composure, and it needed the quiet of the dead body behind him to restore it.

He picked up a telephone and, sitting on the edge of Collinson's desk, called a number. While he waited he whistled a soft, dreamy and abstracted tune, a waltz which probably dated back to the man's youth, for he was middle-aged, with tidy, greying hair and small greying moustache, and his mind might have been less concerned with crime than with jostling memories of the old music halls, of how little Nellie Collins had sung that tune at the Old Bedford, directing her gaze at long moustached gentlemen in boxes decorated with large gold Cupids bearing cornucopias. Yet when he received a reply, he became at once sharply attentive and professional.

'Detective-Inspector Mason speaking. This is Hubert Collinson's house. No, I haven't found what we wanted. Collinson's dead. I arrived too late. Oh yes, murder unquestionably. Will you send one of our best men down? Is Collins on night duty? Well then, send Groves.'

He slammed down the receiver and, crossing to the window, called to a constable who had appeared at a heavy, lumbering run at the end of the street. Once again the professional air slipped from him and he sat down on the desk with a melancholy that seemed connected with nothing so tangible as a dead man.

He gave the impression of being a little disgusted with

his surroundings, as his eye roved here and roved there, and when his gaze lit for a moment on the bookcase and its rows of yellow-backed novels, his smile was almost a malignant grin. Yet, watching the small wrinkles at the corners of his eyes and the almost surly twist of his upper lip, one would have said that chiefly he was disappointed with himself.

The explanation was to be found, perhaps, in the first words he spoke as the door opened and admitted a heavily-built constable with slightly protuberant eyes. 'I am Detective-Inspector Mason of Scotland Yard,' he said. 'I came just too late,' and he waved his hand perfunctorily at the body in the chair.

'Gaw!' the constable said, dragging the monosyllable out to the length of an alexandrine. He stood in the doorway and stared.

'Come, my man,' Mason said with a kind of irritable amusement, 'have you never seen a body before?'

'Never, sir. This is a respectable neighbourhood.' The man drew a deep breath and became suddenly excited and garrulous. 'This is the first chance I've 'ad, sir, of what you'd call a real crime. They put me in these parts because they said the criminal classes would never stand for my eyes.'

'Try a little iodine every day in a glass of milk.'

'I beg your pardon, sir?'

'Exophthalmic goitre. It doesn't make you very bright, does it? Why haven't you asked me for my papers? I'm not a resident of this respectable suburb.'

'But you said, sir . . .'

'Of course I said. But here I am alone with a dead

body. The forms, constable, must be observed. Look through these papers.'

The constable examined them with an air of profound apology, but became suddenly attentive over one of them. 'A search warrant, sir?'

'Yes, he has escaped me, you see.' Mason turned round and, for almost the first time, took a long look at the body. 'Have a good look at this man, constable; look at the way he carries his bald head as a badge of respectability.'

The detective put his finger under the dead man's chin and jerked the face upwards. He bit his lip as he did so, his professional nonchalance punctured by the astonished stare of the eyes that seemed aware of this last breach of respect.

Mason sighed. 'Well, I suppose we must hunt his murderer, but Collinson deserved all that he got. Blackmail,' he added, 'and women.'

'All the same, sir,' the constable said, 'as I see it, bad men aren't always killed for a good reason.'

'Why, constable,' Mason swung round, 'you are a philosopher. And you are right. How right,' he added in a thoughtful murmur.

The constable was encouraged by the praise. 'This is a chance for me, you know, sir,' he said.

'A very small chance, constable. You've been reading fiction, I'm afraid. One of my brightest young men will soon be on his way here in a car from Scotland Yard. How did the murderer escape?'

'The window, sir.'

'It could hardly have been the chimney, could it?' Mason retorted with nervous irritation. He crossed the room and looked over the window-sill. 'An easy way down a drain-pipe. We'll examine that later for scratches. And how about the door? Was it locked by Collinson or the murderer? Search the man's pockets.'

While the constable obeyed, Mason strolled slowly round the room, examining the pictures on the walls, the books on the shelves, the liver-coloured wallpaper, the highly polished mahogany furniture with the same faint, abstracted interest as a man shows who revisits his old home and sees, less the present flames in the fire than the old dreams beating up the chimney. Yet it must have been the future that veiled Mason's eyes with thought.

'There are no keys here, sir.'

Mason started a little at the voice. 'Then possibly the murderer locked the door and took the key away with him.'

He turned to the dead man's desk and laid his hand on a large wooden box. 'You might begin going through these files, constable. They are probably only bills and receipts.'

'It's locked, sir.'

'Then that's more promising. Break it open. We won't waste time looking for the key. Probably business letters, constable, but there, when your business is blackmail . . . And note this. The murderer hasn't touched it, but of course he may have heard me on the stairs. This is a curious case, constable. I seem to have arrived too soon. If I had arrived later he might have left more clues. No, no, you must put on gloves. There is always the chance of fingerprints.'

Again he began to whistle the same waltz, as though it was connected in his mind in some peculiar way with the idea of death.

'Receipts and bills, sir,' the constable said.

'Shop or private individuals?'

'They all seem shops. I'll just begin at the other end, sir, for luck.'

Mason was at the window. 'That fast car from Scotland Yard, constable. I wonder where it is now. Tearing through this hell of a black night. Saunders will be at the wheel and young Groves beside him. That's a keen young man, constable, and intelligent too. This body will call him as a carrot calls a donkey. There's a big difference between the young and the middle-aged. He's got all his bodies before him, and I've got them all behind. When this business is over, constable, I shall retire from active service.'

The pile of letters in front of the constable grew. 'Take to private inquiries, sir?'

Mason laughed, still with a faint undertone of an elegiac melancholy. 'Oh, I've begun those already, constable.'

'I beg pardon, sir?' The constable raised shocked eyes.

'No, no, I don't mean the same as you. Do you know, I have a feeling about this case. I believe the man is going to prove too clever for us. Motive? I expect there are five hundred men, and as many women, with a motive. The road apparently empty below, you on another part of your beat, I on the stairs, all the respectable inhabitants of this respectable suburb in their respectable beds.

'And then look at the knife he's used. A kind sold by the fifty thousand. A fingerprint, perhaps, though he's clever enough surely to have worn gloves. And in any case, he may not belong to the criminal class. One of these respectable sleepers, perhaps, constable.'

Mason began to whistle gently to himself, bathed in a melancholy peace. Collinson's bald head gleamed softly in the electric light, and if he were to bend towards it, Mason thought that he might very well see his own face reflected in its surface. It made him feel as though the dead man were an old and trusted friend, and trusted surely he must have been throughout his life, trusted to do the wrong, the evil thing.

What must the man have felt and thought when alone? It was difficult for frail human nature to avoid some dangerous lapses into virtue, yet Mason was aware of no such lapse in Collinson. Yet how could he have regarded his life when he was alone, when his evil was not whipped up by a client's challenge to his cunning? He must, Mason considered, have invented some tale to satisfy himself, some laudatory belief in his own superhuman power. But he lay there in a crouched attitude, humble and astonished. Private inquiries, Mason thought – certainly I have taken them up.

'By Jove, sir, we've got it.' Mason turned and, with fingers trembling a very little with excitement, took the paper that the constable held towards him. When he saw the familiar writing, the room became a little misty and impalpable, swayed round him, so that the mahogany bookcase, the mirrors, the chairs, turned thin and transparent and waved before his eyes like threadbare banners. It was some moments before he could read the writing.

'If you will not see me,' the letter began abruptly, but there could be no doubt that it was addressed to Collinson, 'I will wait on your doorstep and beat you in the street.' It was signed Arthur Callum and bore no date.

'There's nothing else, sir,' the constable said.

'Wait.' Mason removed his eyes with difficulty from the scrap of cheap notepaper that had so evidently been bought in a 2d. packet together with half a dozen envelopes. If he thought hard, he could even make a guess at the small stationers where Arthur Callum would have bought it, one of those stationers whose single window is filled with an untidy medley of objects – bottles of ink, paper clips, address stamps, notebooks, china ornaments, pens, pencils, fancy penwipers. 'So you think this is a clue, constable?'

'Well, sir,' the constable gazed at his superior with amazement, 'the man seems to 'ave 'ad a grudge.'

Mason seemed in no hurry to follow up the trail, and the constable, dreams of promotion flowing through his mind, thought regretfully of the fast car from Scotland Yard tearing nearer through the night.

'Constable,' Mason said slowly, 'didn't you say just now that even bad men were seldom murdered for a good reason? Surely this letter comes from a man with a good reason. You don't beat a man in the street for a disgraceful motive. Look at this letter, too. Why, man, the ink has faded. The letter may have been written years ago.'

'Why did 'e keep it in this box, sir, ready to the 'and? 'E might 'ave been going to show it to someone tonight.'

Mason said slowly, 'I'll tell you why I'm hesitating. I

knew Arthur Callum well once. I have not met him, though, for many years,' he added, with an enhancement of that surly twist at the corner of his upper lip. 'My friend – he was my friend – was not capable of this,' but the constable noticed that Mason did not look at the body but at the open window.

A solitary taxi hooted dismally in the street below and a small spatter of rain blew into the room.

'Still, sir, it's the only clue we've got. If we could knock up this man Callum quickly . . . 'E wouldn't expect us on the trail so early. We might find something. You know where 'e lives, sir?' He was pleading with voice and with protuberant eyes, pleading for a chance – the only chance that he might ever be given – of praise and promotion.

He had reached that dead afternoon of life when a man is not young enough to recommend himself by his enthusiasm nor old enough to be resigned by any form of sunset touch. Mason's eyes relented a little; he was moved in spite of himself by the man's pitiable inadequacy.

'You mean,' he said, 'that we should have a look at Callum now before Groves arrives?'

'Do you know where 'e lives, sir?' The constable's voice was trembling a little with excitement and with hope.

'Very close. That again is a curious coincidence, isn't it?' Mason smiled with a kind of grim melancholy. 'It certainly would be amazing, wouldn't it, to solve the whole mystery before Groves arrives.'

He added, with a sudden nervous beating of one hand on the desk, 'I hate these clever young men with their complete lack of understanding. Right, constable, I prom-

ise you. We'll surprise him.' Mason raised the letter very
close to his face, as though middle age had already gripped
his sight and made it fail. 'One last look, constable.'

2

Until he saw again the uncarpeted polished yellow deal,
he thought that he had forgotten the appearance of the
stairs, but now his mind ran to the opposite extreme
and he believed that he could recall every scratch and
indentation in the wood, perhaps even its cause. At the
top of the stairs he found the door of Arthur Callum's
room unlocked.

He pushed it open and was for a moment startled by
the familiarity of an engraving over the mantelpiece that
represented the raising of Lazarus from the dead. The
artist had thrown a melodramatic skill into the bearded
face's agony, which might be because of the life to which
he returned or because of the death from which he came.
The table was as Mason had always known it, littered
with books and papers. He smiled a little at what he knew
was the symbol rather than the reality of work. Behind
the table a curtain shut off the corner of the room that
contained Callum's bed.

Mason shut the door softly behind him and turned
quickly, with the air of a man facing an enemy whom he
mistrusted. And mistrust he did, every feature in the
room: the shabby armchair, the leather tobacco pouch on
the mantelpiece, the pipe rack, the row of second-hand
medical handbooks, the large-eyed stare of the familiar
clock. They spoke to him in syllables as measured as
the slow beat of time upbraiding him for his intrusion,

blaming him for the accumulation of the years between them. 'Callum,' he called in a low voice, 'Callum.'

It may have been because he was staring again at bearded Lazarus that he did not see the curtains part and was faced suddenly with the accomplished fact of Callum standing before him. The years that had altered Mason's face, with a deft line here to mark surliness and there to mark melancholy, had apparently left Arthur Callum young, young but ill, pale and with eyes too dark for health.

Again it needed no voice to emphasize to Mason how unwelcome he was. Each man stood and stared at the other with such an uninterested dissatisfaction as an ugly man might show to his own image in the glass.

'I am sorry,' Mason said at last, 'that I have looked you up so late.' He spoke as though every word had to force its way through a hostile air. 'Too late,' he thought that he heard Callum echo in the same tone. Mason glanced at the clock. 'After all,' he said with a forced and jocular ease, 'it's not long past midnight, and from my knowledge of you, Callum – ' and then he stopped, faced with his own blank sense of ignorance. Yes, he had once had knowledge, but there were years between them now.

He said gruffly, 'I've just come from Hubert Collinson's house. You knew him?' Callum nodded; and Mason, in an effort to break through that expressionless face which fronted him like an accusation, said quickly, 'He was murdered tonight.' The satisfaction on Callum's face said as plainly as words that the world was all the better for Collinson's death.

'Oh, I admit it,' Mason said, as though the words had been actually spoken; 'but then a bad man,' he used the constable's phrase, 'is not always killed for a good reason.' He waited for Callum to speak, and while he waited may have thought how strangely unprofessional his conduct was. Somewhere a taxi hooted, but it was the only sound, for Callum did not speak.

'You had a good reason, Callum,' Mason said. His tone was less an accusation than an entreaty, for he was beginning to desire poignantly, bitterly and despairingly that Callum had been the murderer, that Collinson should have been killed for a good reason.

'Listen,' he said, 'this is your letter. At least you cannot deny that,' and he fluttered the letter with its fading ink before Callum's face. 'And the knife – I am the only person in the world who knows the knife is yours.'

He remembered Callum's face at the age of fifteen, pressed against the window of an ironmonger's in Camden Town, while his hand closed on the fifteen shillings which could make the knife his. A mixture of adventure, sentimentality, a curious inverted chivalry had made Callum hide his purchase from all but Mason, and lock it in a drawer where it was presently forgotten, even by its owner; but Mason had not forgotten the emblem roughly engraved by Callum on the handle.

'Oh, yes, the knife is yours,' he said again, and would have drifted back into his memories if he had not suddenly felt that Callum had connected his assertion, had whispered, or perhaps only thought intensely, 'was.' 'Anyway, it's in Collinson's body now,' he said with a brusque brutality. If he had meant to startle Callum, he did not succeed.

Mason began to speak again on the subject of the letter. 'I know,' he said, 'that it was written some years ago. I know the cause of it, too. It occurred before we separated.'

He had known all Callum's acts; even his thoughts were not unknown to him. He, too, has been closely acquainted with Rachel Mann, ambitious Rachel Mann. She had had dark hair that curled closely over the ears, and a peculiar combination of ingenious wide eyes and a cynical, or perhaps only shameless, mouth. His knowledge of her now seemed to him to come less from his own experience than from a reflection of her in Callum's mind, a deep and slightly stained reflection as in an antique mirror.

Callum, he remembered, had declared in his characteristic, challenging fashion, that he was ready to serve seven years for Rachel Mann; but long before those years were over he had lost her and not even gained a Leah. Rachel Mann, already at the age of twenty-five, was a woman who knew exactly what she wanted. She wanted Arthur Callum, but not most. She knew that with her looks and with her brains the stage offered her a fine and pleasantly notorious career. She wanted above all things to be talked about.

Mr Hubert Collinson at that time was largely interested in various theatrical enterprises, and he was also, when she introduced herself to him, interested in Rachel Mann. It was really only Arthur Callum who objected to the form the interest took, and the objections that led him to threaten Hubert Collinson crumbled with many other things when he found that he was too late.

And yet Mason knew very well that the first impetuous anger had something transiently fine in it that had nothing to do with jealousy. Indeed, there was never any reason for jealousy, Rachel Mann considered her relations with Mr Hubert Collinson in a purely business light, while she was genuinely, though intermittently, fond of Arthur Callum.

Mason's face reddened suddenly in a jealous rage against Hubert Collinson. Have I not said that he also had known Rachel Mann? It was unbearable to think that the dead man, with his bald head and his lifeless and imbecile air of surprise, had once discovered all the secrets which an intimacy with Rachel Mann must have held, even a businesslike intimacy.

It was unbearable to know that up till an hour ago Mr Hubert Collinson had been at liberty, whenever he chose, to sit down in his chair and go into his own mind and remember and live over again the scenes – whether passionate or cold could little matter after many years – that he had known with Rachel Mann. And perhaps most unbearable of all was the thought that Hubert Collinson in all probability valued these memories so cheaply he never troubled to recall them. Yet the slightest of them would once have fed Arthur Callum for a lifetime.

Then Mason remembered that this which he was feeling was only jealousy, the rather petty jealousy of a man who had been cheated of something he desired.

Staring at the fading ink, Mason knew that it had not

been a jealous man who had written the letter. Indeed, so little jealous had Callum been that he would have given everything to have married Rachel Mann, even after he learned that she was Collinson's mistress; but Rachel Mann would not marry him.

She had no objection, she explained on one terrible evening, to loving him occasionally; but he had neither the money nor the influence to make her a good husband, and apparently not seeing how her words affected him, she offered him her love then and there, not as he had once dreamed and hoped and longed and fought for, for a lifetime, but for three-quarters of an hour before she dined with Collinson.

'And now I suppose, when you think of it,' Mason said slowly and with disgust, as though he assumed that Callum had been able to follow his thoughts, 'you wish that you had accepted that three-quarters of an hour. Then there would have been a memory to share with Collinson. Why,' he went on in a bitter, almost hysterical, outburst, 'instead of killing Collinson, you could have sat together over your wine and swopped your memories.'

Then he remembered how certain he was that Arthur Callum was not the murderer. The certainty pained him. 'Why didn't you kill him,' he implored rather than asked, 'twenty years ago? You had a good reason.'

The phrase sang in Mason's head, along with the constable's utterance. For a long time now he had forgotten that he was Detective Inspector Mason of New Scotland Yard, forgotten the waiting policeman with the hopeful, protuberant eyes, and young, intelligent Groves in his fast car tearing through dark, deserted streets and nameless suburbs.

Callum's impeccability began to seem to Mason a re-flection on himself. What right had Callum to claim, even by this silent facing of accusation, an honesty and a chivalry that he, Mason, did not share? But the anger passed quickly and only the hopeless longing remained, the longing that Callum might have been the murderer, that the reason for Collinson's death might have had something in it fine and unselfish and fearless.

'Suppose,' he caught himself saying, and surely it was an odd way for a detective to address a man whom he had come to arrest, so odd that Mason himself smiled and thought that indeed the time had come for him to retire and to take up private inquiries; 'suppose you had killed him, then, when you wrote this letter? Why, man, you wouldn't have hanged. No jury would have convicted you. You needn't have been afraid.'

But he knew very well that in those days Arthur Callum would not have been affected by fear. 'You fool,' he said, 'you silly, romantic young fool, to let a woman like Rachel Mann break you up. If it was a woman you wanted, couldn't you have gone into Piccadilly and chosen one just as pretty and far less expensive? It all comes down to biology in the end. Now,' he waved his hand in a tired, halting fashion, 'look at the mess you've made. Oh yes, it's you, Callum, and not I, Mason, who have made the mess.'

A sudden burst of wind drove the rain in a loud flurry against the window, and Mason's nerves showed themselves in his start. He turned to face the night and as he did so there sprang into his vision again the clock, the mantelpiece, the risen Lazarus. But there was no need surely for these to affect him. These did not belong to the Callum whom he had once known so intimately; they had only been hung round him by an attentive landlady.

But though they did not belong, like a jewel that has lain long in one place, they had left their mark on the living flesh; their imprint was a part of Callum now, as much a part of him as those things which were wholly Callum's, though he, Mason, had once shared them – a long, dark, overhung lane of dripping trees, and the faint, fresh smell of rain; a river in which the reflection of stars and street lamps were inextricably mingled; a sleeping woman's face; and the sound of a voice singing in the sun behind a hill beside the sea.

Pain spread through Mason's body and brain and heart, until the small room, with its four walls shutting him in, seemed an instrument of lifelong torture, each wall to which he turned reflecting the same memories, despairs, regrets, each wall a mirror that, he protested, distorted, and yet he knew sought out the unexaggerated truth in his heart, and when he shut his eyes, ceiling and floor shut him in the closer with the same message.

Though perhaps, to open the door and go meant the end of this long torture, he hesitated, for at least there was silence in which a man could think, and although thought hurt, any thought was better than the noise and action which waited for him without – the hooting of a car, the spatters of rain, excited voices, whistles blowing in the night, the ring of telephone bells, feet pounding on the stairs. 'Motive? The man was a blackmailer. He had pressed someone too hard. Someone who had a great deal to lose.' The wrong reason.

Callum's silence seemed to be asking him a question. 'Arrest you?' Mason cried. 'I wish I could. Why, I can't even bring you back.' Back now to noise and action and worry and the responsibility of decisions. He flung Callum's door open, passed outside, slammed it behind him, and turned to face a flight of yellow deal stairs, still undisturbed and silent, and standing on the top step, her black dress fading into the dark, her white face only evident, Rachel Mann.

There were many reasons why Mason could not have expected thus to meet her, yet he felt no more surprise than a man feels at the incongruity of some of the images that drift through the unthinking mind. She was there. That was clear in the black sweep of her hair round the ears and the slightly open, slightly pouting lips, their tint a little more vivid than nature had intended.

She, like Arthur Callum, seemed to have remained young during all the years that had jostled Mason this way and that way, pushing him down paths which he had never foreseen and making him a little older, a little more filled with disgust at the ways of himself and the world. It was unfair that during all that time Rachel Mann should have kept her beauty.

'Hubert Collinson is dead,' he said to her in a tone purely conversational, as though he thought the news might interest her, as indeed it should have interested Collinson's former mistress. A long band of yellow light from a street lamp outside fell between them, and the band was constantly speckled and its appearance altered by the invisible gusts of rain which beat irregularly against the glass of the lamp.

It gave the impression of a constant flow and eddy of small objects, and emphasized their own immobility in their patches of shadow. It was as though the tossing years had at last left them still and stranded on separate beaches.

'It should have happened before or never at all,' he added. He was beginning to discover how very frayed his nerves were. He was continually giving way to inexplicable outbursts, less of rage than a kind of nagging elderly rancour. 'Oh, it will surprise you,' he continued, 'to hear that you were not concerned, that you had nothing to do with it, that, Rachel, you were of no importance whatever. Hubert Collinson was murdered for quite another reason.'

His eyes clouded and the storm of his nerves for a moment subsided. 'Yes, you were the right reason, Rachel. Why couldn't you have been what Callum thought you were – worth while? Why didn't you marry him? You don't understand Callum, Rachel. I know him better than does anyone else in the world, so you must let me tell you about him. He's a scientist gone wrong. He wanted to be a doctor because he had a passionate devotion to a sentimental idea of service. But he hasn't a clear enough idea of what he wants to serve. He thought it was you, and now it will narrow down to himself. Rachel, you and I know how deadly dull that last is. You and I. You and I.' The phrase continued to echo on in his mind long after the words had faded out, but still the woman made no movement, whether of pity, horror or surprise.

'But you are responsible, yes, you are responsible,' Mason broke out again. 'It's you who broke Callum. Collinson had to die. We both of us know that. But he needn't have died for a wrong reason.' He was infuriated by her silence and calm. It seemed to him a form of conceit. 'I am Rachel Mann and nothing that anyone may say or do can affect me. Bluster, be bitter, be pitiful, sinful, virtuous. I shall feel not the faintest reflection.'

There had always been something of that attitude in her, the germ, so to speak, of the present great calm, as the youngest and loveliest body bears in it the germ, however small, of death. 'Yes, it's you who have killed Collinson,' he continued in a quieter tone, for loud words seemed less able than silence to cross the gentle eddy and flow in the stream of light between them. 'If it were not for you, Callum would never have met Collinson.'

He thought that he saw her eyes alter very slightly into a polite, mechanical, uninterested question. 'Oh no, I'm not going to arrest him.' He waved his hand. 'He's safe enough back there, but I mustn't forget *myself* just because he doesn't belong, any more than you belong, to this hour and place. Rachel, suppose' – the word rang in his brain like a cracked bell set swinging in a deserted house – 'suppose you had married Callum.'

A succession of images swayed through his mind, of days and nights of a great passion, tenderness and continually of peace. He forgot for a short moment how irrevocably the present had arrived, that Collinson was dead and his death must inevitably involve another.

He forgot the days during which he had watched the

slow disintegration of his own character, the growing self-disgust, deceit and corruption, he forgot even that he was Detective-Inspector Mason of New Scotland Yard and remembered only a night when he had faced Rachel Mann as he faced her now and said, with the same trembling passion, clinging to a hope which he knew but would not admit was illusory, 'Rachel, marry me.'

The patch of polished yellow deal lit by the streaming light glimmered more brightly, dissolved, became a glass through which he again could see the surroundings of Callum's room, the table, the scattered books, the tortured face of Lazarus hanging from the wall, and Rachel Mann alone with him in the room. The stillness of her face altered a very little, the eyes glanced over his shoulder at the clock, the lips began to open, trembled on the verge of their infamous proposal.

Mason winced in the expectation of pain, and then the years swept between and brushed away the face and the lips which were about to speak words that seemed no longer infamous, but an amusing and satisfying suggestion, for after all everything came down to biology in the end, he reflected, and began to laugh.

3

He was still laughing as he lowered the letter and faced again the constable's impatient and protuberant eyes. Between them the electric light on Hubert Collinson's desk shed a soft carpet of gold, and behind the policeman's head Hubert Collinson's clock showed that two more minutes, valuable for their loneliness and for the absence of young intelligent Groves, had fled. He was beginning to feel an affection for the constable, so closely thrown together were they by their isolation and by the mute witness of their contact.

'Oh no, constable,' he said, the relics of laughter making his voice tremble, 'Callum is not the man we want.'

'No, sir?' The eyes goggled with disappointment but remained filled with a childlike faith in the prescience of Scotland Yard.

'For the last few minutes, constable, I have been holding private inquiries.'

'Yes, sir?'

'And I have come to the conclusion, constable, that you are going to have your triumph over Groves. A spectacular triumph. Look, we have eight minutes still, and the air is full of clues.'

'I thought you said, sir, you arrived too soon.'

'I've changed my mind. Listen, constable, luck favours you. I happen to know that this letter was written more than fifteen years ago, and the quarrel concerned a woman. You can take my word for it – I knew both Callum and the woman very well – that the quarrel has been dead for almost as long as the letter has lain in Collinson's files. All this I know. Now you must spin your theories, constable. What is the most likely cause of the murder?'

'Blackmail, sir, I should say.'

'And you would also say that the murderer had a certain position to lose to make him sufficiently desperate for this, or even to make him worth blackmailing. That disposes of Callum, constable, a penniless medical student. I can see that you are a sharp man, and you are saying to yourself that the murderer is probably an elderly man. He would not otherwise, unless born with a silver spoon, be high enough game for Collinson. An aristocrat or an elderly man, then, is not too wild a surmise.' Mason found now that his nerves were quite steady, and he was enjoying the last game of his professional career. 'Now look at the knife, constable. What do you notice?'

'There's a kind of badge engraved on it, sir, amateur work, sir, I should say.'

'That doesn't matter. Look at the angle of the knife.'

'It's very crooked, sir.'

'The man who struck that blow put his body's weight into it. He couldn't trust the strength of his wrist, you see. Yes, an elderly man, constable, or else a very effete aristocrat.'

He laughed at the admiration in the policeman's eyes. The man evidently believed that he was face to face with the detective of fiction, the detective of lightning deductions. 'Has the origin ever occurred to you, constable,' he said – it amused him to delay his own inquiries, to play cat and mouse with the slipping minutes – 'of Sherlock Holmes's cleverness? It's simply that the author knows the answer and works backwards. That's what I'm doing.'

'You know the answer, sir?' The policeman's admiration, far from diminishing, had increased.

'Yes, I know the answer, but you must discover it for yourself. This is your chance. You have still six minutes. Now tell me again how the murderer escaped.'

'Out of the window, sir.'

'Any scratches on the window-sill? No, but then of course he may have worn soft shoes. Come and look out of the window. A convenient drain-pipe and a thirty foot fall. We could have done it easily enough when we were young, but now – this is a moment for elegiacs, constable. We have decided that he was probably an elderly man.'

'If 'e'd 'eard you on the stairs, 'e'd 'ave risked it, sir.'

'True. Remember he was a man with a weak wrist. He should have fallen hard in the flower bed underneath. Run down and see if you can find footprints.'

While the policeman was out of the room, Mason strolled around it, with a sour disgust at his own sentiment, looking for any relics of Rachel Mann. This, he thought, is the damnable result of private inquiries. The sooner he was done with the whole business the better. Well, in five minutes Groves would have arrived and the past could hand over worry, searchings, danger, boredom, and perhaps corruption too, to the future.

Still, as his thoughts wandered, his eyes were awake for any signs of Collinson's former mistress. Admirable men, he said to himself, there are none. Rachel Mann had gone and left Collinson with a smoking-room story. The close black hair and the impetuous mouth had become a tale a little scented with the smell of whisky. What a lot of trouble would have been saved if Rachel Mann had left Callum with no more majestic a memory.

Mason began to feel a little tired, though the calmness which had followed his thoughts of stormy 'might have beens' endured. He welcomed the return of the constable as an indication of the passage of time. The game was losing a little of its savour, though it still amused him to think that his last service in a professional capacity would be to a suburban police constable hungry for promotion.

'There are no marks, sir.' The constable's face was puzzled and anxious.

'No, I thought not. You must alter your theory, constable.'

'This is the top floor. 'E couldn't 'ave gone upstairs, sir.' The man's hand suddenly clenched and he lowered his voice. 'You don't mean 'e's in the room now, sir, hiding?'

'In that big cupboard, for instance? Oh no, I hardly think he's there. What do you think about the key, man?'

'The key?'

'The one that isn't in Collinson's pocket, of course. The one that locked the door.'

'Well, sir, Collinson might have locked it, so's 'e could be alone with the man.'

'But why should the man take it?'

'It might've been 'im as locked the door.'

'Yes, on the inside or the outside.'

'Well, sir, if it was on the outside 'e'd 'ave met you.'

'But, man, if it was on the inside, where is he?'

The constable looked round him helplessly. His shoulders drooped a little as he saw the clock. The fast car from Scotland Yard might arrive at any moment now, and he was no nearer the promotion for which opportunity had so desperately awakened his ambitions. He turned to the window, less with the idea of finding any clue than of listening for the car which would end his hopes, and presented to Mason's gaze a greying patch of hair.

Mason expressed a faint sigh of exasperated pity and put his hand into his hip pocket. The policeman, his eyes blurred with self-commiseration, his ears straining to detect through the constant spatter of the rain what he believed was the distant 'burr' of an engine, heard a sudden metallic clatter on the floor and turned. On the floor between him and Mason lay a key.

The policeman remained silent, staring at it, unable to grasp its significance. Only when Mason said sharply, 'Well?' a look of mingled anxiety and fear came into the policeman's eyes. 'You found it, sir?' he asked in slow, puzzled tones, his head drooping towards the key, as though it possessed magnetic power.

Mason let himself down on Collinson's desk with some difficulty. The moment of retirement had come and he felt his age acutely. It was that, indeed, and the disgust and disappointment with himself induced by memory, that had led him to shrink from all the trouble and anxiety and useless strain of deceit which would have as its only result the preservation of life for a few more insignificant years. He could not, however, try as he would, keep his voice to the casual, uninterested note which he desired. It sounded to himself taut and quivering.

'You see, constable, the murderer escaped by the door and locked it behind him. Then he broke in and found the body. May I lend you my handcuffs, constable?' and Mason held them out on the palm of the hand. When the constable remained speechless and stupidly staring, Mason grew impatient.

'Damn you, man, move to it,' he said. 'I hear a car.' As

the policeman, still silent and with fumbling shocked fingers fitted the handcuffs on to his superior's wrists, Mason spoke again.

'The credit really belongs to you constable, because you found Arthur Callum's letter, and I was once Arthur Callum. But this murder had nothing to do with Callum. I only wish it had. You don't see a jealous lover here, constable, only an elderly, corrupt police officer who has killed his blackmailer. As you said, a bad man's not always killed for a good reason. Listen, there's the car.'

He turned his back to the door at the sound of light, running feet up the stairs, and Groves was faced, as he entered, only by the white face and protuberant eyes of the police constable and the bald, tip-tilted head of Hubert Collinson and his stare of astonishment.

'You've come too late, Groves,' Mason said, still with his back turned. 'The mystery has been solved without you,' and turning suddenly, he held out his handcuffed wrists in a theatrical gesture which he could not resist. 'Oh no, it's not a mistake,' he added. 'It would have been the perfect murder, Groves, but for this constable. I commend him to you.'

He walked to Hubert Collinson's desk, fixing his eyes on it as though, like a drunken man, he was anxious to assert the straightness of his gait. Actually it was to banish from any absurd visions there might be of a relenting or a pitying Rachel Mann.

Groves, a young alert man in a light mackintosh and a bowler hat, said slowly, 'I don't understand. Is this some sort of joke?'

'Come now' – Mason still spoke to the two men as though he were their superior officer – 'you must take my statement,' and not waiting on their stumbling efforts to find pencil and paper, he began to recite in a slow, controlled voice an exact account of his movements and his motive. Even the motive, and his awareness that it was indeed the wrong reason, seemed not to trouble him now.

It was his listeners who were troubled, his listeners reflected many times in the obtrusive mirrors of Hubert Collinson's flat, and later his more numerous listeners at the Old Bailey, judge, jury, counsel; but Rachel Mann remained untroubled, for she had been dead for ten years, and the voice was nothing if it was not terrestrial.

An Appointment with the General

She felt the unprofessional shyness that she always experienced, with a sense of inadequacy, before an interview – she lacked, as she well knew, the brazen front of the traditional male reporter, but not, or so at this time she still believed, his cynicism – she could be as cynical as any man and with reason.

She found herself now surrounded in the small courtyard of a white suburban villa with half-Indian faces. The men all carried revolvers on their belts and one had a walkie-talk which he kept pressed closely to his ear as though he were waiting with the intensity of a priest for one of his Indian gods to proclaim something. The men are as strange to me, she thought, as the Indians must have seemed to Columbus five centuries ago. The camouflage of their uniforms was like painted designs on naked skin. She said, 'I don't speak Spanish,' as Columbus might have said, 'I don't speak Indian.' She then tried them with French – that was no good – and after that with English, which had been her mother's tongue, but that was no good either. 'I am Marie-Claire Duval. I have an appointment with the General.'

One of the men – an officer – laughed, and at his laugh she wanted to walk straight out of the courtyard, to make her way back to the pseudo-luxury of her hotel, to the half-finished airport, to take the whole dreary way back to Paris. Fear always made her angry. She said, 'Go and

(138)

tell the General that I am here,' but, of course, no one would understand what she was saying.

One soldier sat on a bench cleaning his automatic. He was stubby and grey-haired. He wore his uniform with the stripes of a sergeant carelessly as though it was just a raincoat which he had huddled on against the thin vagrant rain which was blowing up now from the Pacific. She watched him closely as he cleaned his gun, but he didn't laugh, while the man with the walkie-talk continued to listen to his god and paid her no attention at all.

'Gringo,' the officer said.

'I am not a gringo. I am French,' but of course she knew by this time that he didn't understand any word she said – except gringo. He accused her again with his mocking smile – or so she believed because she didn't speak Spanish. All women, he seemed to be saying to her, were inferior if they hadn't a protector and she was more inferior than most because she spoke no Spanish.

'The General,' she repeated, 'the General,' knowing that she pronounced the word all wrong for a Spaniard, and she fished out of the poor memory she always had for foreign names that of the General's adviser who had made this appointment for her, 'Señor Martinez,' wondering all the time whether the name was right – perhaps it was Rodriguez or Gonzalez or Fernandez.

The sergeant snapped back the chamber of his automatic and spoke to her in almost perfect English from his bench. 'You're Mademoiselle Duval?' he asked.

'Madame Duval,' she said.

'Oh, you're married then?'

'Yes.'

'Well, it doesn't much matter,' he said, and he set his safety catch.

'It does to me.'

'I wasn't thinking of you,' he said. He got up and spoke to the officer. Although by his stripes he was only a sergeant, he had a kind of unmilitary authority about him. She found his manner a little insolent, but he was equally insolent to the officer. He swung his automatic to indicate the door of the small unimportant suburban house. 'You can go in,' he said. 'The General will see you.'

'Is Señor Martinez here – to translate?'

'No. The General wants me to translate. He wants to see you alone.'

'Then how can you translate?'

His smile, she noticed, after all was quite free from insolence in spite of the words he used. 'Ah, but here we say to a girl, "Come with me to be alone."'

She was stopped short again just inside a little hall which contained a bad picture, an occasional table, a nude statue of the late Victorian kind and a life-size china dog, by a soldier who pointed at the tape recorder which was slung over her shoulder.

'Yes,' the sergeant said, 'it would be better if you left that on the table.'

'It's only a recorder. I never learned shorthand. Does it look like a bomb?'

'No. All the same – it would be better. Please.'

She laid it down. She thought, I'll have to trust to my memory, my damnable memory, the memory I hate.

'After all,' she said, 'if I am an assassin you have your gun.'

'A gun is no defence,' he told her.

2

It was more than a month since the editor had invited her to lunch at Fouquet's. She had never met him, but he sent her a neat and courteous letter stamped out in a type which resembled book printing, praising an interview which she had published in another journal. Perhaps the letter read a little condescendingly, as though he were conscious of controlling a review of a higher intellectual grading than the one in which she wrote. It would certainly pay less, always the sign of quality. She accepted his invitation because the morning it arrived she had had one more 'final' quarrel with her husband – the fourth in four years. The first two had been the least damaging – jealousy after all is a form of love; the third was a furious quarrel with all the pain of broken promises, but the fourth was the worst, without love or anger, with just the irritated tiredness that comes from a repeated grievance, from the conviction that the man one lives with is unchangeable, and the sad knowledge that she didn't care much anyway any more. This one *was* the final quarrel she thought. All that was left for her now was the packing of suitcases. Thank God there were no children to consider.

She came into Fouquet's ten minutes late. She had been kept waiting in restaurants far too often to be punctual. She asked the waiter for Monsieur Jacques Durand's table and saw a man rise to greet her. He was tall and lean and very good-looking – in that he reminded her of her husband. Good looks could be as nauseating as chocolate truffle. He would have had an air of almost overpowering distinction if his greying hair had been a little less well waved over his ears, though the ears, she admitted, were the right masculine size. (She disliked small ears.) She would have taken him for a diplomat if she had not known him to be the editor of that distinguished left-wing weekly which she had seldom read, not being in sympathy with its tendency towards modish politics. Many men who at first sight seem dead come alive in their eyes: but in his case it was the eyes which were the deadest part of him, in spite of their condescending gallantry: only in the gestures of his elegant carcass as he seated her beside him and handed her the menu did he come to a sort of life – a seductive life but a seduction which expressed itself only with words.

He suggested that it would be best if they took the turbot, and when she agreed he told her again in exactly the same phrases that he had used in the letter, how much pleasure her last interview had given him, so perhaps the words really were his and not his secretary's – he would hardly have learnt her words by heart. He added, 'The turbot here is very good.'

'Thank you. It's very kind of you.'

'I've been noticing your work for a long time now, Madame Duval. You get below the surface. Your interviews are not dictated by your victims.'

'I use a tape recorder,' she said.

'I didn't mean literally.' He crackled his toast melba. 'For a long time now, you know,' – his vocabulary seemed limited, perhaps by the rules of journalistic protocol – 'I have thought of you as one of us.' Obviously he meant the statement to be a compliment and he paused, probably waiting for her to repeat 'Thank you'. She wondered how long it would be before he began to talk real business. The suitcases were yawning emptily on her bed. She wanted to fill them before her husband returned – it was unlikely, but not impossible, that he would return before dinner.

'Do you know Spanish?' Monsieur Durand asked.

'French and English are my only languages.'

'Not German? Your interview with Helmut Schmidt was beautiful – and so destructive.'

'He speaks English well.'

'I doubt if the General does.' He fell silent over his turbot. It was very good turbot, one of Fouquet's specialities. She thought, 'If I can get out of the apartment before Jean returns it will save a lot of argument.' Argument could be left later to the two *avocats*. There would have to be, she supposed, a meeting of *conciliation* – the thought bored her profoundly. She wanted as quickly as possible to wipe the whole slate clean.

'The situation in Jamaica is another subject I have in mind. You could pick up Jamaica on your way out. You said you speak English, didn't you? A rather more sympathetic approach perhaps to Manley than you are used to. He's one of us, even though for the moment he's "out". The General, I think could be a subject in your usual style. Suitable for your brand of irony. As you can imagine we don't much care for generals – especially Latin-American generals.'

She asked, 'You mean you want to send me somewhere?'

'Well, yes. You are a very attractive woman. And by all accounts the General likes attractive women.'

'Doesn't Manley?' she asked.

'I wish you spoke a little Spanish. You have such a valuable knack of asking the right personal question. Politics, we believe, should never make dull reading. You are not under contract, are you?'

'No, but what General? You don't want me to go to Chile, do you?'

'We are getting a little tired of Chile. I doubt if even you could be very fresh on the subject of Pinochet – and would he receive you? The advantage of a really small republic is that it can be covered – in depth mind you – in a matter of weeks. We can regard it as a microcosm of Latin America. The conflict with the United States, of course, is more in the open there – because of the bases.'

She looked at her watch. She was wondering if she could get all she wanted for the moment into two suitcases – to go where? 'What bases?' She would not leave a note because it could be used by lawyers.

'The American, of course.'

'You want me to interview the President? Of what republic?'

'Not the President. The General. The President doesn't really count. The General is chief of the revolution.' He poured her out another half-glass of wine. She had only ordered a small carafe. 'You see we are a little bit suspicious of the General. It's true that he has visited Fidel, and that he met Tito at Colombo. But we wonder whether his socialism is not rather skin-deep. He is no Marxist certainly. Your method with Schmidt would suit him admirably. And perhaps on the way there or back a sympathetic portrait of Manley in Jamaica. We feel quite happy about Manley.'

She was still not sure what country it was he wanted her to visit. Geography was not her strong point. Perhaps he *had* mentioned the name, but if he had it had dropped out of sight into the empty suitcases. Anyway it didn't really matter: anywhere was preferable at the moment to Paris. She said, 'When is it you want me to go?'

'As soon as possible. You see there may be a crisis in the next few months, and if that happens . . . you might find yourself only writing the General's obituary.'

'A dead General, I suppose, would certainly not be a socialist good enough for you.'

His laugh, if it could really be called a laugh, was like the scraping of a dry throat, and his eyes, which were now fixed on the menu, the turbot having been meticulously finished, showed no sign that a joke, like an angel, had passed quietly overhead and vanished. 'Oh, as I said, we are rather doubtful about his kind of socialism. May I suggest a little cheese?'

3

'You might find yourself writing his obituary' – the phrase spoken two weeks ago by a modish left-wing editor over the Fouquet menu – came immediately back to Marie-Claire's mind when she encountered the tired and doom-laden eyes of the General. Death was the accepted premature end, she had always understood, for generals in Latin America; the alternative might of course be

Miami, but she couldn't see the man before her in Miami, sharing that city with the ex-President of the Republic and the ex-President's wife and his brother-in-law and cousin. Miami was known here, she had already learnt that, as 'The Valley of the Fallen'. The General was dressed in pyjamas and bedroom slippers and his hair was tousled in a boyish way, but no boy would have had eyes so laden with the future. He spoke to her in Spanish and the sergeant translated with correct though rather stiff English.

'The General says you are very welcome in the Republic. He does not know the paper for which you write, but Señor Martinez has told him that it is very well known in France for its liberal views.'

Marie-Claire believed in provocation; Helmut Schmidt had responded promptly with anger and pride, to her first questions, he had given himself away to the merciless tape, but the tape this time had been left behind in the recorder. She said, 'No, not liberal – left-wing. Would it be true to say that the General is much criticized for moving so very reluctantly towards socialism?'

She watched the sergeant closely as he translated, trying to attach a meaning to the Latin-sounding words, and his eyes twinkled back at her as though he were amused at the question and perhaps approved it.

'My General says he is going where his people tell him to go.'

'Or is it the Americans who tell him?'

'My General says that naturally he has to take the Americans into account, that is politics in a country as small as ours, but he need not accept their views. He suggests that you must be tired of standing: you should make yourself comfortable in the armchair.'

Marie-Claire sat down. She felt the General had scored over Helmut Schmidt – and over herself too. She hadn't yet had time to think of her next question – she had expected the General to leave a door open for her to make a quick impromptu question, but he seemed to have closed all doors firmly in her face. There was a long and awkward pause; she was relieved when the General spoke again.

'My General says that he hopes Señor Martinez is helping you in every way he can.'

'Señor Martinez has very kindly lent me his own car, but the chauffeur speaks only Spanish which makes it difficult for me.'

The two of them began to discuss together what she had said at some length. The General slipped off one shoe and stroked his left sole.

'My General says you may dismiss the car and the chauffeur. He has given me orders to look after you – Sergeant Gurdián is my name. I am to take you wherever you may wish to go.'

'Señor Martinez asked me in his letter to make out a programme for him to approve.' Again there was a consultation.

'My General says it is best for you not to have a programme. A programme kills.'

The tired and brooding eyes watched her with what she took to be amusement like those of a chess player who knows that he has made a surprise move and disconcerted his opponent.

'My General says that even a political programme kills. Your editor ought to know that.'

'Señor Martinez thought that I should visit . . .'

'My General says you should always do the opposite of whatever Señor Martinez advises.'

'But I was told that he was Chief Adviser to the General.'

The sergeant shrugged his shoulders and smiled too. 'My General says that while, of course, it is *his* duty to listen to his advisers, it is not *your* duty.'

The General began to talk in a low voice to the sergeant. Marie-Claire had an impression that the interview was slipping disastrously out of her hands. When she had abandoned the recorder she had abandoned her best weapon.

'My General wants to know if your editor is a Marxist.'

'Oh, he supports the Marxists – in a way, but he would never admit to being one himself. Before the war people used to call his type a fellow-traveller. The Communist Party is legal here, isn't it?'

'Yes, it is quite legal to be a Communist. But we have no parties.'

'Not even one?'

'Not one. A man can think what he likes. Is that true in a party?'

She said – and she meant it to be an insult – for in her experience it was only when a man became angry that he told the truth – even Schmidt had told a few truths – 'Is your General a fellow-traveller like my editor?'

The General gave her an encouraging smile, and for a

moment he looked a little less tired, a little more interested. 'My General says the Communists are for a while travelling on the same train as he is. So are the socialists. But it is he who is driving the train. It is he who will decide at what station to stop, and not his passengers.'

'Passengers usually have tickets for certain destinations.'

'My General says he will be able to explain more easily to you when you have seen something of his country. My General would like before you return to Europe to see for once his country through your eyes. A stranger's eyes. He says they are very beautiful ones.'

So the editor was right, she thought, he likes women, he finds women easy, power is an obvious aphrodisiac . . . Charm too can be an aphrodisiac, Jean had plenty of charm, he had exuded charm with the skill of a politician, but she was finished with charm and aphrodisiacs. She said, 'Now that the General has power, I suppose he finds women easy to come by.' Sergeant Gurdián smiled. He didn't translate.

'I suppose he enjoys his power,' she said. She nearly added, 'And his women.'

She tried a question which she had sometimes found worked surprisingly well. 'What does he dream of? At night I mean. Does he dream of women?' She continued with mockery, 'Or does he dream of the terms he is going to make with the gringos?' The tired and wounded eyes looked at the wall behind her. She could even understand the single phrase he spoke in reply to her question. '*La muerte.*'

(149)

'He dreams of death,' the sergeant translated unnecessarily, and I could build an article on that, she thought with self-hatred.